Trudy's Island Holiday

Trudy's Island Holiday

Mary A. Faid

Marshall Pickering

Pickering and Inglis
Marshall Pickering
3 Beggarwood Lane, Basingstoke, Hants RG23 7LP, UK

Copyright © 1950 by Mary Alice Faid
Originally published in 1950
Reprinted 1960, 1967
This edition published in 1986 by Pickering and Inglis Ltd
Part of the Marshall Pickering Holdings Group
A subsidiary of the Zondervan Corporation

ISBN 0 551 82372 2

Printed in Great Britain by
Hazell Watson & Viney Ltd
Member of the BPCC Group
Aylesbury, Bucks

CONTENTS

CHAPTER I

They Arrive at the Island

THE yellow-funnelled steamer cut her way through the blue water, leaving a frothy line of foam behind her. It was summer and the sun was shining. The steamer's deck was crowded with happy people all wearing bright, expectant faces; but perhaps the happiest of all were the four young folk who were gathered near the stern.

The Lawsons were off on holiday. As their parents were not long home from a long stay at the seaside for the good of their father's health, it had been decided to let the young ones holiday on their own.

Ping, the youngest, was kneeling up on his seat, his eyes on the foamy track of the steamer. Beside him, her dark hair blown about her face, sat thirteen-year-old Nancy. She was listening to the cries of the gulls and the swishing of the waves and thinking that these things made music, though it was a different kind of music from the piano at home.

Seventeen-year-old David, standing at the rail, had other thoughts, for his was the eye of the artist. His heart thrilled to a distant view of purple hills against the skyline, wreathed by a cluster of feathery clouds.

And what was Trudy thinking about as she stood by his side, her red-gold hair fluffed about by the breeze and a rapt expression on her face?

She would have replied that she was not thinking

at all, only dreaming. All this beauty and freshness, with the prospect of three weeks' holiday, was filling her with happy anticipation. At the same time, she could not help wishing that it might be possible for everybody less fortunate than herself to share her experience.

"What a lot of soap there is down there!" exclaimed Ping in a high, excited voice.

"That's not soap, it's foam," laughed Nancy.

"Well, it looks like soap." He turned to Trudy. "How long will it be till we get to the island, True?"

"About an hour. Then we've got half an hour in the bus to Ardensheel."

Ping had been disappointed at first, on learning that Barone Island had people on it. He would have preferred an uninhabited spot where he could have lived like Robinson Crusoe. However, he and David were going to camp out in a field, instead of staying at the farm with Nancy and Trudy, which was an exciting prospect for a small boy.

Gradually the line of hills drew nearer and they could see a rocky shore and a bay round which houses were clustered against a background of trees. This was Dunglas Bay, where they were to disembark.

As the steamer came closer to the pier, each of them took their portion of the luggage. Ropes were thrown on the pier, the gangway was lowered, and the four Lawsons soon found themselves walking up towards a turnstile at which they each paid a penny.

Dunglas Bay was a good-sized resort, with a patch of sand bordered by a row of bathing boxes. Mothers sat round, knitting and reading, while their children ran about, in and out of the water.

An old man rattled out some cheerful music on a barrel-organ, and there was quite a bustle on the promenade. At the top of the pier stood an old red bus with a board near it which said:

ROUND THE ISLAND.

David, who was in charge, bundled them all on to it. Ping would have liked to stay to buy ice-cream, but there was no time to spare.

"Two and two halves to Ardeensheel," David asked the conductor when they had started.

It was the most breath-taking run any of them had ever had. At first the road was level and ran beside the beach. Then they began to climb. Below them were cliffs falling sheer to the water. Hair-pin bends and switchback curves kept them in a state of excitement. Above, they could see purple moorlands rising to jagged peaks. David's eyes glistened:

"What a place to live in and paint pictures!" He had brought his sketch book and paints, but what artist could hope to capture the beauty of all this?

Every now and again the bus would stop at some farm or road-end to deliver parcels and disembark passengers. Nancy chattered on, and so did Ping, but Trudy, as was her habit when deeply moved, kept silent. It had been good of her mother to arrange this holiday for them. It was because of her own memories of Ardensheel, where she had holidayed as a girl, that she had written to the farm to ask if they could board her family. Yes, was the reply, they could give the girls a small room and supply a tent for the boys who could have their meals in the house. A few other guests would be staying, which was all the better, thought Trudy.

Miss Stewart of the farm had promised to mother them, but the Lawsons were an independent family, used to looking after themselves.

Having run along a road bordered by tall trees whose branches met overhead, the bus ran through a tiny village and came to a halt beside a narrow lane.

"This is your stop," the conductor told them. "Go up the lane and you will see a yellow house across the fields. That's Ardensheel Farm."

Heavily laden, they panted along the lane, which came to an end at the gate of a field and there, sure enough, was a big yellow house surrounded by small out-buildings. With the sun's rays on it, it almost dazzled their eyes. In front, at the foot of a steep decline, lay a deep cove with shining pebbles, on which was drawn up a sturdy rowing-boat.

"Goody!" shouted Ping. "Do you think they'll let us go out in the boat, David?"

"Wait and see," he was told.

They passed in through the gate and across the field-path, eyeing doubtfully several munching cows, but the docile animals took no notice of them, and they reached the door unmolested. It was lying open, and as David put up his hand to ring the bell, a middle-aged woman in a dark frock and floral apron, came forward, smiling.

"I suppose you are the Lawsons." Her voice had a musical lilt. "I remember your mother very well. I was just a girl, too, in those days."

This, then, was Miss Stewart. She took Trudy and Nancy upstairs to a tiny room with two windows, one a skylight in the roof, and the other facing the sea. The ceiling sloped down at one side above the bed, and Trudy told herself she would have to be careful not to bump her head when she sat up in the morning.

There was a wardrobe, a small dressing-table, and two chairs. Everything was neat and clean, and the place would look quite homelike, once their possessions were unpacked.

"I'm busy with afternoon tea," explained Miss Stewart. "If you come down for it now, the boys can see about their camp afterwards."

They were only too willing to obey, as the meal on board steamer had by no means satisfied them.

The four of them were shown to a small table in the middle of the dining-room. The other guests looked up as they entered and Trudy smiled at them rather self-consciously.

Later, as they sampled the light meal of sandwiches and home-made scones, she took courage to look about her.

There were two other tables in the room. The one in the corner was occupied by three people; a sad-eyed couple who looked like man and wife, and a slim, dark, young lady whose beautiful hair was streaked with silver. She sat very quietly, staring ahead of her as if her mind were far away.

At the window table, an elderly, aristocratic-looking woman with forbidding features was talking in a low voice to a little girl about the same age as Ping. The child was dressed in a silk frock with white shoes and socks, very spotless and fine, but not the kind of attire for a place like this. Trudy and Nancy were wearing simple print frocks, and in their cases were short skirts and jerseys that would stand up to all sorts of adventures on the beach and hills.

Ping leaned over to say, in a whisper:

"That little girl looks like an angel, doesn't she?"

Trudy smiled, but saw his point. The child's face, lit by a pair of huge blue eyes, had a frail, appealing look, and her hair hung in long, golden ringlets over her shoulders.

There was such a subdued atmosphere in the room that the Lawsons felt unusually tongue-tied.

Tea over, the occupants of the corner table moved out, and they heard the little girl say:

"May I be excused, Grandma?"

At a regal nod from the old lady, she slid off her chair and walked towards the door. She halted, however, to have a good look at Ping as she passed.

"Hello," said he. "What's your name, little girl?"

"Eva," she whispered, "Eva Somers. What's yours?" But before Ping could answer, her grandmother spoke sharply: "Eva, dear, go upstairs *at once*."

The child gave her a scared look and obeyed immediately. So, thought Trudy, it seems that Eva's grandmother does not approve of us. The idea worried her. She hated snobbery, and was sorry for Eva, who seemed a lonely little mite.

But Ping was in a hurry to see their camping quarters. Miss Stewart took them through the kitchen to a shed at the back. With the help of Andy, the 'orra man,' who did odd jobs on the farm, they got out the ground-sheet and tent, and followed Andy across the field to a sheltered spot beside a burn.

While the boys erected the tent, Trudy climbed up to a ridge above, and exclaimed with surprise at the view.

"There's a beautiful sandy bay down there on the other side," she called. "That means we're on a peninsula!"

"What's a peninsula?" shouted Ping.

"Don't you know yet? A piece of land almost surrounded by water. Come and have a look, Nancy!"

Nancy scrambled up beside her. To the left they could see the peninsula tapering off in a heap of jagged cliffs. Before them was this beautiful sandy bay, and behind lay the pebbly cove. On the right stretched green fields rising up to moors and hills. What a beautiful world it was, and how thankful they should be for the power to enjoy it!

"If we're allowed to use the boat, we'll be able to row right round the peninsula," said David, joining them.

"There's sure to be caves and things." Ping was at his elbow. "And look—fishing boats!"

At the far end of the bay they could see the masts of several boats lying together. Beside them was a collection of huts and cottages.

"That must be Waterside. I saw it on the map," declared David. "A famous artist lives there in the summer. Brian Clyde."

"Never heard of him," sniffed Nancy.

"Oh, you never heard of anybody. Wouldn't it be thrilling if we should meet him?"

"It's not likely he would look at us even if we did," she replied.

At this point, Ping suddenly became conscious of the state of his inside.

"I'm simply starvishing! When do we get something to eat?"

Realizing that it must be nearly supper time, they made a bee-line for the farm. On the way, Trudy said reflectively:

"Isn't it queer, Nancy; those folk we saw at tea-time must have been here for a day or so at least. You would think that seeing all this beauty would make them feel happy. Yet they don't look happy, not one of them."

"Perhaps they don't see the beauty. Perhaps they've got something on their minds that blinds them to it."

"I believe you're right. I wonder what's wrong with them all? I don't suppose we shall ever know."

In that she was wrong, for during the days to come, they were to be brought into very close contact with their fellow-guests.

Supper was served at seven and consisted of a two-course meal which they all enjoyed, especially the creamy milk at dessert. When it was over, Ping looked sleepy, so they all went out again to the tent to tuck him up for the night. The boys each had a straw palliasse, and there were plenty of blankets, so there was no doubt about their comfort.

In spite of his excitement at the novelty of sleeping in a tent, Ping did not forget to say his prayers. Trudy sat beside him, as she had done many a time when their mother was away, and listened to the long list of 'blesses' which he always included. To-night, he commended to God all the new people they had met, even to Andy the orra man and the little girl who 'looked like an angel.' There was a plaintive note in his voice when he added:

"And please, God, bless my Mum and Dad and

my pussy-cat Abednego, and don't let him think that I have forsaken him." It was a sore point with him that he had not been allowed to bring his cat with him.

After tucking him in, Trudy gave him a good-night kiss which he allowed because there was nobody looking. David said he would stay around. Already he had out his sketch-book and was sharpening his pencils, although the light was beginning to fade.

Nancy yawned. "I'm feeling sleepy, too. Race you back to the house, True!"

The two set off, hair blowing in the wind, sandalled feet scarcely touching the ground. The air was so fresh and strong they felt as if they could run for miles. But when they got back to their little bedroom, Nancy was glad to take off her clothes and lay her head on the pillow.

Trudy, however, was too full of thoughts to go to bed and sleep. In spite of her fondness for company, there were times when she liked to be alone. For a while she stood at the window, watching the waves lapping over the pebbles in the cove, and the limitless expanse of sea and sky. Then she tip-toed from the room and went downstairs.

Intending to ask Miss Stewart if she had any books that she might read, she knocked at what she thought was the kitchen door, opening it when she heard a voice say: "Come in!"

Entering, she was amazed to find that she had mistaken the room. This place was like a little parlour, except that there was a bed in it, and sitting up smiling at her was the owner of the voice she had heard. Round her shoulders was a grey shawl of Shetland wool. She was elderly, with silver hair smoothed back from a centre parting. Her face was very placid, and the eyes which looked at Trudy were of a clear, forget-me-not blue.

"Come right in," she urged. "It's not often I have a visitor."

As she shyly approached the bed, Trudy became aware that the atmosphere in this room was wonderfully peaceful and that the old woman's face had a radiance on it that seemed to come straight from heaven.

CHAPTER II

The 'Stella Maris'

I'M very sorry," said Trudy, as she looked into the old woman's smiling face. "I thought this was the kitchen."

"I'm only too pleased to see you, lassie. Are you one of the new guests?"

"Yes. My name's Trudy Lawson. I'm here with my two brothers and my sister."

"Ay. Your mother was just your age when she used to come here. I mind her fine. A bonnie lass. And her daughter is bonnie too."

"Oh, no." Trudy blushed. "I could never be like my mother, neither in looks or anything else."

"Well, you're shaping well, anyway. I suppose you'll have heard her speaking about me? I'm Mrs. Stewart."

"Yes, she often tells me how kind you were to her, in spite of your being kept so busy with the farm."

"Ay, it was a busy life, but it's all past for me now. I haven't been able to walk this ten years or more."

Trudy's voice was very gentle when she asked:

"Was it an accident?"

"Ay, that's just what it was; a fall from a haystack. But don't look so upset, child, I've got used to the idea of being helpless. Since I've been shut up in this wee room, I've had far more blessing than ever before.   Won't you sit down and tell me about yourself?"

Trudy took a chair by the bedside.   The window faced west and the rays of the setting sun were shining in, lighting up the walls of the room and falling on the large framed photograph of a young man with thick, wavy hair and a laughing face. Trudy wondered if it was Mrs. Stewart's son of whom she had heard her mother speak.

Below the picture stood an old organ; and all the other furnishings were old-world and mellow, which perhaps accounted for the peacefulness of the room.

As a rule, Trudy was not a great talker.   By nature, she was dreamy and thoughtful and when she did express her feelings it was only to her closest friends.   But there was something about the room and her companion's eagerness to listen which loosened her tongue.   She found herself telling Mrs. Stewart about the family, her friends, and the school in Drumleigh.   She even confided a little of her aspirations for the future.

"So you intend to be a school-teacher?   It's a very fine ambition.   One of our guests here is a schoolmaster—Mr. Cooper."

"I think I saw him and his wife in the dining-room," replied Trudy.   "They looked rather sad, I thought."

"Yes.   They were here last year too, but they had their little girl Jennifer with them then.   She died during the winter, and my daughter tells me they are broken-hearted."

Trudy felt very sorry for the Coopers.

"And that lady who sits with them, is she a relation?"

"No, I don't think so. That must be Miss Winton. I don't know anything about her."

"She's very pretty, but she doesn't look happy either. She just seems to me as if she had lost all interest in life."

Mrs. Stewart smiled.

"So you're an observer of human nature, are you? And what do you think of 'Lady' Somers? That's what my daughter Polly calls her, because she's so high and mighty."

"Oh, dear, yes. She nipped us off nicely at tea."

"Ay, so she would. The little girl came running in here one day, but her grandmother soon called her back. I heard her being ordered never to do it again. Her parents are in India, I believe. Her father is a tea-planter there, but the child was sent home as the climate did not agree with her. She looks very frail, but I think if she was allowed to run wild a little it would be the life of her."

Trudy agreed. After some more talk, she was about to take her leave, when Mrs. Stewart asked:

"I wonder if you would do something for me, dear, before you go? My eyes aren't as good as they used to be, and Polly's far too busy these days to read to me." She brought out a Bible from below her pillow. "If you would read the fifty-fifth Psalm——?"

Trudy obeyed willingly. She read the Psalm through in a clear, steady voice. When she had finished, the invalid repeated a phrase in a low tone:

"'Cast thy burden upon the Lord and He shall sustain thee'. I've found out the truth of that during these years, Trudy. If only all those that had burdens would take to heart these words!

You read the Bible well, lassie, as if you were used to doing it."

"I am used to it," replied Trudy. "My mother brought us all up to read our Bibles and to believe in God and Jesus Christ, our Saviour."

"I'm very pleased to hear it, my dear. We share a wonderful secret, don't we?" She took Trudy's hand in her frail one. "I feel as if I want to share my secret with the whole world, but what can an old woman do, shut up in a little room? It's young folk like you, with all your faculties, that can spread the good news."

"I know," said Trudy. "I do try, Mrs. Stewart."

"I'm sure you do. Even in a place like this, there are chances to show people where the true road to happiness lies. You mustn't forget that, even though you are on holiday, Trudy."

"No," she promised, "I'll not forget."

As she was leaving the room, her eyes lingered on the photograph on the wall.

"Is he your son?" she enquired shyly.

"Ay, that is Donald. He went his own ways, many years ago. He was a wayward laddie, and maybe his father was a bit hard on him. I pray to God every night that some day he will come back home again."

Impulsively, Trudy went over to the bed and kissed her. "I'm sure your prayers will be answered," she said.

Then she left the room closing the door softly behind her. She was glad now that she had made the mistake of going into the wrong room, to become acquainted with this brave old lady, who could face her troubles with such courage.

The evening was so warm that she stepped out

of doors into the garden and sat down on a seat near the open window of the lounge, to think about what Mrs. Stewart had said to her. By and by, she heard voices in the room.

"It's a lovely night, Agnes." It was Mr. Cooper speaking. "Wouldn't you like to come for a walk?"

"No, thank you, I don't feel like it." His wife's voice was cold and indifferent.

"It might do you good. You used to enjoy walking at this time."

"Don't speak to me about what I used to do! You know very well I'll never enjoy walking, or anything else, again. Perhaps you would like me to forget about—Jennifer?"

Her husband replied soothingly:

"No, of course not. I loved Jennifer too, Agnes, but I'm sure she would hate to see us unhappy like this. Life must go on, you know."

Trudy was on her feet, unwilling to hear any more, but the bitter words of Mrs. Cooper followed her as she walked away:

"Speak for yourself! Perhaps your life can go on, but mine can't. I might as well be dead—"

Trudy had never heard the voice of such grief before. She felt sick and sorry for the mother who had lost her child, but she was sorry for the father too. How terrible that his wife should have shut her heart to him. Surely trouble such as theirs should have brought them together instead of driving them apart?

Then she thought of the calm faith of Mrs. Stewart, her courage and fortitude. How different these two women were; and why? It was not difficult to guess. The one had the love of God in her heart, while the other's was empty and cold.

Shortly afterwards she returned to the house and went upstairs to the bedroom. Nancy was sound asleep at the front of the bed, so that she had to climb over her to snuggle in at the back, under the low ceiling. It was getting dark now and the sky-light window shone palely above her. All she could hear was the swish of waves in the creek and the occasional call of a sea-bird. It was all very different from the noise of the traffic which went on till all hours at home.

Usually, when she went to bed, her mind went over the affairs of the day, but to-night she was so drowsy with the sea air that her eyes closed immediately and she knew nothing more till she heard a persistent knocking at the door.

It took her a few moments to realize where she was. A wonderful brightness was in the room, the golden light of the morning sun. Nancy's dark head was dug into the pillow. She was still fast asleep.

"Come in!" called Trudy.

The handle was turned, and Ping entered the room, carrying in his arms a brown puppy with liquid eyes and a small, intelligent face.

"Look, Trudy, this is Rusty. He's two months old and he's got two brothers and his mother is called Kelpie, and Andy says I can look after him while I'm here." He took a deep breath. "Hurry and get up, you pair of lazy bones! It's eight o'clock and David and I have been up for AGES!"

He laid the puppy on the bed beside Trudy.

"He's lovely," she conceded, "but is this the right place for him?" She yawned. "How did you and David get on?"

"All right. I just woke once and heard a big

thing scuffling round the tent. I thought it was a tiger, but it turned out to be just a cow." He sounded disappointed. "David and I had a bathe from the sandy beach."

Nancy was awake now.

"Brrr. Wasn't it cold?"

"Yes, but I splashed about and soon got warm. David's teaching me to swim."

"Run along then, Ping. I want to get up," Trudy told him. He lifted the puppy, cuddling it in his arms.

"I asked Andy about the boat and he said it was for the use of the guests. He says the boating's quite safe, except when there are sharks about."

"Sharks!" Trudy sat up and promptly bumped her head on the ceiling. "Ow, that was *sore*! Nancy, you can jolly well sleep at the back to-night; my skull's precious. What's this about sharks?"

"Well, Andy says sometimes there's a school of sharks in these waters; isn't it exciting? There's been none for a while, though. They call them basking sharks."

"M'm, I've heard of them. They're not dangerous, though, not like the man-eating sharks."

"Perhaps there might be man-eating sharks too," he suggested hopefully, as he went out of the room.

While she dressed, Trudy told Nancy about the new friend she had made last night.

"Poor old thing," commented Nancy. "Imagine having to lie like that, doing nothing and seeing nobody. I think I'd rather be dead."

"But she doesn't take it like that. She's quite cheerful, even though her son ran away from home years ago. What about coming in with me to see her to-night?"

"Oh, Trudy, you know I haven't got a bedside manner like you."

Trudy laughed. "It's a wonder then, for you're fond enough of your bed. Come on, show a leg! I'm going to look for the bathroom. Breakfast's at eight-thirty!"

When the gong rang, Trudy was ready dressed in a scarlet jumper and pleated navy skirt. As she entered the swing door of the dining-room, Mr. Cooper held it open for her with a pleasant greeting. His wife was already at the table with Miss Winton, who looked ill and unslept.

Ping and David were already seated.

"I'm starvishing," complained the small boy.

"Hush, Ping, that's not polite."

"Can't I get a holiday from being polite?"

"No," David told him. "Remember the folk here will judge you from your manners."

"I hate manners," Ping shuffled about in his chair. "They're not the real *Me*."

"Then you should practise them till they are the real *You*, and you'll never be caught out," advised his brother.

Ping's attention was diverted by the entrance of Mrs. Somers and Eva. The old lady, distant as ever, went to her seat without glancing round, but Eva sent a shy smile in Ping's direction. Her shell-pink frock was delicate and spotless, and her bright hair was tied with a pink bow to match.

The last person to come down was Nancy. She sat down breathlessly, as a plump, smiling maid was handing round plates of porridge.

"That's a bad mark for you," commented Ping.

"Mum said we must always be in time for meals."

Instead of replying, Nancy turned to David:

"Let's go out in the boat after breakfast. I'm dying for a swim, and I've always wanted to dive off a boat."

After getting permission from Miss Stewart, they carried the oars out of the shed and raced excitedly down to the creek where the boat lay. It was old, but broad in the beam and sturdily built. Round the inside of the stern was printed the name: *Stella Maris*.

"That's Latin for 'Star of the Sea.'" Trudy was keen to air her knowledge.

"Ay." Andy the orra man was at their heels. "It was Master Donald who called her that."

Donald, the missing son of the house. How had he ever been able to tear himself away from this beautiful place which he must have loved deeply?

Andy helped David to push the boat down the beach

"You will be all right in the boat, Master David, but the lassies are not to take her out alone; she's too heavy."

The girls promised to obey and were about to step into the *Stella Maris*, when Ping ran down, saying: "Eva's up there, and she wants to come with us. Say she can, Trudy!"

The pleading figure of the little girl could be seen at the gate.

"I'm afraid her grandmother wouldn't be pleased," replied Trudy.

"Ask her, then. She's in the lounge; I saw her."

Reluctantly, Trudy retraced her steps to the house. She did not feel at all sure of her reception, and yet Eva seemed so lonely it seemed a pity not to take her with them.

She found Mrs. Somers writing a letter, and made her request. The old lady looked up, scandalized.

"Eva go for a sail in that disreputable rowing-boat? I should think not!"

"We'd take good care of her, Mrs. Somers. My brother knows all about boats."

"Perhaps, but my grand-daughter is delicate. I definitely forbid her to go. In any case, we don't know you. Please send Eva to me here."

There was nothing more to be said. Trudy ran back to the beach. When Eva heard of her grand-mother's decision, tears filled her big blue eyes, and she turned sadly away.

"It's a horrid shame," muttered Ping indignantly.

"Yes, I'm sorry for that kid," said Trudy. "Evidently she's not going to be allowed to have anything to do with us."

They took their seats in the boat, Ping at the bow, the two girls in the stern, and David at the oars. Andy gave them a good push off and David rowed out, quite pleased to display his skill. Eva watched them, waving forlornly. As they passed on they could see Miss Winton sitting among the rocks, her eyes lowered over the book she was reading.

"I don't believe she knows she's at the seaside," declared Nancy. "She might as well be locked in a prison cell."

"Perhaps she is," said Trudy unexpectedly. David gave her a look. He knew what she meant. Miss Winton might be free enough in body, but she gave one the impression that her spirit was caged and dark.

"I wish I could set her free," was Trudy's un-spoken thought.

CHAPTER III

Music on the Waters

DAVID rowed them towards the end of the peninsula which was called Rocky Point. In fairly shallow water, Nancy, who had put on her bathing costume, dived from the boat and raced them ashore. Patches of firm sand lay between the rocks and they pulled the boat well up where the tide could not reach her. Though Trudy was not a swimmer like her sister, she soon joined her in the water, while David took out his sketch-book to to make a study of the scene. Ping, meanwhile, started to scramble among the rocks on a tour of exploration. Soon he let out a shout of triumph.

"Whoops, there, I've found a cave!"

Nancy ran up, all dripping. "Show me where!"

Ping led her through a narrow alley of rock to a gaping hole in the cliff.

"It's a real cave. It goes ever so far in. And look, Nancy, here's a fireplace. Somebody must have lived here. Suppose it was an escaped convict?"

"More like a tramp," sniffed Nancy.

Ping stayed by the cave exploring the inmost recesses where it was very dark and damp, with water dripping from the slimy walls. He was quite glad to come out into the daylight again and to see David busy with his pencil, and his sisters sitting on the rocks like a couple of mermaids. While he stood there, very still, he was sure he heard music.

It was the sound of singing, coming from across the bay, and he actually knew the tune.

> Fierce raged the tempest o'er the deep,
> Watch did Thine anxious servants keep,
> But Thou wast wrapt in guileless sleep,
>   Calm and still.

The others had heard it too. It was coming from the direction of the cottages at Waterside.

"The fishermen must be holding a meeting," said David.

"What a funny time to hold a meeting!" exclaimed Ping.

David explained that, as the fishermen were out in their boats from sunset till dawn, they couldn't very well have a meeting at night.

"Take us there in the boat, David!"

David looked at his watch and found it was time to hurry back for lunch.

"To-morrow, perhaps," he said.

There was a scramble for the boat which was now heavier to pull, as the current was against them. When at length they reached the cove they could hear the lunch-bell ringing.

"Bad marks for everybody!" cried Ping as they raced up the beach. By the time they had tidied themselves and got downstairs again the diners had reached the second course and Trudy felt rather ashamed. She made a vow not to let it happen again.

Mr. Cooper smiled across at them and they could see Eva eyeing them, in spite of her grandmother's warning looks.

"Been having a good time?" asked Mr. Cooper.

"Yes, thanks, we found a cave," replied Ping, and Eva's eyes grew big.

After lunch, Trudy sat out on the lawn to write a letter to her mother. She told her about their fellow guests and old Mrs. Stewart, and about what they had been doing since they came.

"This is the most beautiful place I have ever been in, Mum. It is a shame to see sadness among such beauty, but some of the people here are not very happy, I'm afraid. I'd love to be able to do something for them. I will, if the opportunity arises.

"We are getting sunburned already. Ping has about a million more freckles since you saw him, and Nancy's nose is cheerfully red. David's tan is quite aristocratic, but I'm afraid my schoolgirl complexion is totally ruined. Ping sends his love to you both, and to Abednego. That cat would be very jealous if he could see Rusty, a farm puppy whom Ping has adopted. It's just as well they are far apart. I'll have to finish now to catch the post. We are going to the Silver Beach this afternoon, across the fields——"

They found the Silver Beach a fascinating place. There was a long stretch of sand shelving up to grassy dunes sheltered from the wind. In one of these they parked their gear; Trudy took out her book and David went off to sketch. For Nancy and Ping the sea called again, and soon Trudy was lost to the world, following the adventures of 'Jo' in 'Good Wives,' which Miss Stewart had lent her.

She came back to reality when a shadow fell across her book and she looked up to see Miss Winton. There was a wistful smile on her pale face.

"Do you mind if I sit down here beside you?" she asked.

"Please do." Trudy spread out David's raincoat, and her fellow-guest sat down with a sigh of relief.

"I've just been for a walk and feel rather tired. You see, I'm just convalescing from an illness."

So that was the reason for her pallor, and perhaps even those grey streaks in her hair.

"The air here should make you strong before long," said Trudy.

"I'm sure I hope so. At the moment I feel as if I'd never be strong again."

"I'm sure that will pass, Miss Winton."

"You're very comforting, Trudy. You sound quite motherly. I suppose it's because you're the eldest girl of the family. How old are you?"

"Fifteen," replied Trudy. "Nearly sixteen, really."

"And no doubt that nice head of yours is full of dreams for the future?"

"Of course."

"I was the same at your age. I had great ambitions." Her voice was rather bitter.

"What were they?" Trudy asked with interest.

"I wanted to be a singer. My voice was trained by the best teachers and I worked very hard. I was actually started on my career when—something happened."

There was silence for a moment; then she went on: "I took a serious throat trouble, which meant I had to give up all my plans. Now that my hopes have come to nothing I simply don't know what to do with my life."

She said the words in a whisper, almost as if she had forgotten Trudy's presence. Trudy was at a loss how to reply.

After a silence Miss Winton spoke again.

"Forgive me for worrying you, Trudy. You should be thinking of nothing but happy things, at your age."

"But, Miss Winton, there's so much trouble in the world, how could I possibly not think of it? My mother says we should be ready for trouble when it comes; that we should build ourselves a Security against all the troubles that may arise."

"Yes, I suppose that is the ideal way. She must be a good woman, your mother. My parents used to think like that, too, when they were alive. When I was a child I went to Sunday School and sang hymns, but I gave up such things long ago. I came to have faith only in myself; and now I've lost it——"

Trudy felt heart-sorry for her.

"Miss Winton," she said impulsively, "I think it might do you good if you had a talk with Mrs. Stewart. She's an invalid, you know, confined to her bed." And she told her the circumstances.

"I didn't know that. Yes, I'll certainly go in and see her. Not that I think her religion has anything for me, but I'm sure she must feel lonely lying there."

They were interrupted by the intrusion of no less a person than Mrs. Somers, in a state of great agitation.

"So here you are, Miss Trudy Lawson. Why can't you keep a watch on that young brother of yours? He'll have my little granddaughter drowned before he's finished!"

Trudy got quickly to her feet. Down there in the shallow water, Ping and Eva were wading happily, Eva with her fine clothes tucked up, her sweet young voice ringing with laughter.

"But they're doing no harm, Mrs. Somers!"

"That child ought not to get her feet wet. She's delicate, I tell you."

"Salt water is supposed to be good for you," observed Miss Winton.

Mrs. Somers glared at her.

"I know what is best for Eva, thank you. I've called to her, but she doesn't seem to hear." She turned to Trudy: "Please go and fetch her!"

Trudy ran down towards the two children. Eva's hair, usually so tidy, was blown about her face, and her pink frock was splashed with water, but how she was enjoying herself!

"Your grandmother wants you, Eva. Ping, you shouldn't have encouraged her to go into the water."

"I didn't encourage her. She wanted to!"

"I'm not coming out!" exclaimed Eva. "I like having bare feet. I never want to wear shoes again!"

It took Trudy some time to persuade her to obey. The pretty face scowled when her grandmother forbade her to go into the water again. Trudy felt the old lady was making a mistake to go against the child's natural desires, but she could do nothing whatever about it.

It was now time for them all to go back for tea. On the way across the fields they met Mr. Cooper who had been for a visit to Waterside. His wife he said, was lying down with a headache.

David, who had also joined them, asked him if he knew anything about Brian Clyde, the painter.

"Yes, indeed. I've just seen his house—the outside, of course. I don't know him personally. They say he holds meetings for the fishermen every forenoon."

"We heard them singing to-day across the bay."

"They were singing, 'Fierce raged the tempest'," put in Ping, "but it wasn't raging at all. I wish it would rage, it would be lots more fun. If we stayed here all the year round we'd have storms and shipwrecks, perhaps even sharks."

"Who wants sharks?" asked Nancy. "I prefer to swim without them nosing around. Come on, everybody, I'll race you to the stile!"

They all accepted the challenge except Miss Winton and Mrs. Somers. Mr. Cooper arrived first. He seemed to be enjoying himself. Seeing that Eva was last he went back for her and gave her a pick-a-back to the house. The air rang with her gleeful shouts.

Mrs. Cooper must have recovered for she was sitting on the lawn. When she saw her husband approach, prancing like a horse, with Eva on his back, she rose to her feet and stood waiting with a strange expression on her face.

"Put the child down, Robert," she said sharply; "her grandmother will object."

Stopping short, he placed Eva on the ground without a word. Trudy saw the little incident and guessed that it hurt Mrs. Cooper to see her husband play with Eva as he used to play with their own little girl. Because she was unhappy herself she grudged happiness to others.

Trudy felt the impulse to follow her into the house and try to say something that might remove some of her bitterness, but she did not know her well enough. She made up her mind, however, that if the chance arose she would do her best to break down the barriers and become her friend.

CHAPTER IV

Olivia Winton and Others

THAT evening, after saying good-night to the boys in their tent, Trudy persuaded Nancy to come with her to visit Mrs. Stewart.

She knocked at the door of her room and was told to come in. She had not expected to find anyone else there, and was taken aback by the sight of Mr. Stewart whom she had only seen at a distance hitherto. He was a big, towering man with stern features and a gruff voice, and the girls felt rather shy of him.

However, after nodding to them, he said he would leave them to talk to his wife, and went out of the room.

"Don't look so scared," laughed Mrs. Stewart. "My husband won't eat you. He's not used to bonnie young girls and doesn't know what to say to them."

"I didn't know what to say to him, either," confessed Trudy. "This is my sister, Nancy, Mrs. Stewart."

Nancy took the frail hand in hers.

"She's like you, yet different, Trudy. More of a tomboy, eh?"

"I'm afraid I am," replied Nancy. Her eyes had already scanned the room, noting the old harmonium and the picture above it of Donald Stewart.

"And what have you been doing with yourselves to-day?"

They told her about their sail in the forenoon, and how Ping had found a cave.

"At Rocky Point? Yes, I've heard of it. Donald used to go there, when he was a boy, to play at pirates. Boys love caves, don't they? I don't suppose you've been to Waterside yet?"

"Not yet, but we heard the fishermen singing."

"That would be one of Brian Clyde's meetings. A wonderful man, that. 'The Preaching Artist,' they call him."

"Do you know him?" asked Trudy.

A smile played over the peaceful old face.

"Very well. Before he built that house for himself, Brian used to come here for his holidays. He still comes to see me sometimes. Yes, Trudy, he has been in this room many a time."

"My brother, David, would be thrilled to hear that. He is an art student, you know."

"You seem to be a clever family. What is Nancy's special gift, I wonder?"

Nancy blushed. "I'm not really very clever, Mrs. Stewart."

"Oh, Nancy, you needn't be so modest. You know fine you can play the piano," supplied Trudy.

"Perhaps you could play a tune on the old organ then? It's a long time since it's been played."

"Well, I'll try," said Nancy doubtfully.

She opened the lid and pulled out some stops. After a few wheezy experiments with the pedals, she got well under way and soon was giving quite a good rendering of 'Summer suns are glowing, over land and sea.'

The invalid listened with a pleased smile.

"Thank you, lassie, I enjoyed that very much. Do you think you could play me 'At even when the sun was set'? It's my favourite hymn."

Nancy remembered the hymn very well, and Mrs. Stewart sang with the organ in a sweet, quavering voice:

> At even when the sun was set,
>   The sick, O Lord, around Thee lay;
> O in what divers pain they met!
>   O with what joy they went away!
>
> Once more 'tis eventide, and we,
>   Oppressed with various ills draw near;
> What if Thy form we cannot see,
>   We know and feel that Thou art here.

After the last chord died away there followed a silence, broken by a tap at the door.

"Come in!" called Mrs. Stewart.

Miss Winton came into the room, her arms full of wild flowers.

"I gathered these for you," she said to the invalid. "Trudy told me about you."

Mrs. Stewart took the flowers delightedly, burying her face in their fragrance.

"Wild roses and honeysuckle, the sweetest perfumes in the world. Thank you, my dear. You are Miss Winton, aren't you? That was a very kind thought."

Trudy got a vase from the kitchen and the flowers were placed near the bedside. Trudy had the feeling that Miss Winton and Mrs. Stewart might have more to say to each other if they were alone, so she and Nancy said goodnight and left the room.

Olivia Winton sat down, her sad eyes on the picture of Donald Stewart.

"Is he your son?" she asked.

"Ay, poor Donald. He was always having

words with his father. Ten years ago, he ran away from home. I don't know where he is now. They tell me he was maybe killed in the war, but I'm aye hoping he will come back."

"You loved him very much?"

"He was my only son," said the old woman simply.

"You must be very bitter. Especially having to lie here all day."

"No, I'm not bitter; not now. I've got a lot to be thankful for. I'm well looked after, and I have many kind friends How could I be bitter when God puts it into people's hearts to bring me presents like these flowers you gave me just now?"

"You make me feel ashamed," said Olivia. "I wish I had your peace of mind. I've been very miserable just recently, you know," and she explained how all her hopes for the future had been blighted.

"It seems more than I can bear. I lived for nothing but my singing and my career, and now that I can sing no more, life is a terrible blank!"

"Is it certain you'll never be able to sing again?"

"Not the way I used to. Not well enough to be a success."

"Still," suggested the other, "you may be able to use your voice for some purpose."

Olivia shook her head.

"If I can't have a career, I don't want to sing. You need something else besides a voice, you know. You need singing in your heart, and I'll never have that again."

"Don't be so sure." Mrs. Stewart laid a comforting hand on hers. "I once felt like that myself. But now I always have that 'singing in my heart' you talk about. God puts it there. Whenever I feel downcast, I cry to Him and it is never in vain. He comes into the room beside me and lifts me up, and I feel the singing again."

"That is very lovely," said Olivia wistfully, "but God would not come to me like that!"

"How do you know? Have you ever cried to Him?"

"What's the good?" She rose to her feet. "Religion isn't for people like me."

"Christ's message is for everybody," said the other.

Impulsively, Olivia bent and kissed her.

"I think you are a darling, and I'm coming back to see you soon. Trudy was right. You have done me good."

"Then do come back, my dear, and we'll talk some more." She gave her a bright smile as she left the room.

Then Olivia went for a walk alone under a sky which was dark blue, with a full moon shedding a golden light over the still waters. She was thinking about the old woman and her God, and wishing that she herself could find the same comfort.

From her bedroom window, Trudy watched her as she walked in the moonlight. She was such a lonely person, like a lost sheep looking for a shepherd. She had beauty of character, too, or she would never have thought of bringing Mrs. Stewart those flowers. Trudy felt that here was a strong personality without a purpose; but if a purpose could be infused into it, something great and fine would result.

She prayed that night, in her simple way, that

although the worldly hope Miss Winton had set her heart on had failed her, she might soon find a higher, heavenly hope that would never fail.

Next morning they asked Miss Winton to accompany them in the boat, and she was glad to accept, sitting in the stern with the two girls. Ping was a bit shy, at first. He would rather have had Eva for company, but they knew it was no use approaching her grandmother again.

Miss Winton proved better company than he had hoped. It seemed she had travelled a lot abroad and had actually been in Palestine.

"What were you doing there?" he asked breathlessly.

"Singing to the troops during the war," she told him.

"Then you saw where Jesus lived?"

She nodded, smiling. "I was at the Sea of Galilee."

"What was it like?"

"Not so different from this," was the reply.

He couldn't get over it. "It must be easy for you to be good, when you've seen where Jesus lived."

Miss Winton flushed. "I don't know about that."

"Some day, when I'm a man, I'm going to Palestine, and lots of other countries."

They were rowing in the direction of Waterside. Gradually the cluster of fishermen's cottages became more distinct. At the mouth of the river which ran into the bay, the boats were gathered, sea-gulls wheeling around them. On the hill above stood a fine, white house, not large, but well-built, with a verandah in front and arched windows framed by virginia creeper.

"That must be Brian Clyde's house." David shipped his oars. "And look, there is someone coming down the hill."

They watched the man striding down to the shore. He was very tall, and they could see the sun glinting on his thick, red-gold hair. He wore a white shirt open at the neck, and his arms were bare.

"He's very handsome," murmured Nancy.

"Huh," grunted David. "What does handsome matter? He's a great artist."

"He's good as well as great," added Trudy.

On the beach, the fishermen were gathering from the houses. They stood in a group in their blue jerseys, heads uncovered in the summer sunshine. The air was so clear and still that every word of the service reached them.

The first hymn was very suitable for the occasion:

> When morning gilds the skies,
> My heart awaking cries,
> 'May Jesus Christ be praised!'
> Alike at work and prayer,
> To Jesus I repair,
> 'May Jesus Christ be praised!'

There was something stirring in the fervour with which they sang.

Then Brian Clyde began to speak to them, just as Jesus had done, thought Ping, to His disciples at the Sea of Galilee:

"Blessed are the poor in spirit, for theirs is the Kingdom of heaven. Blessed are they that mourn, for they shall be comforted . . ."

Miss Winton's face was very intent as she listened. Then, as the fishermen bowed their heads, Brian Clyde began to pray. He asked that those who had found God would continue to serve Him and to bring others to Him; and that those in trouble, to whom the world had ceased to appeal, would find happiness and a new life in Him.

He put into words all that Trudy felt in her heart but was unable to express. What did Miss Winton think of it all? Her face was thoughtful, but she made no remark as David rowed them from the scene, his oars dipping gently in the smooth waters of the bay.

There was no time to visit Rocky Point this forenoon, but David promised to row them there to-morrow. He wanted to go back to the spot himself to finish his sketch, and planned to go there this afternoon by foot round the shore.

When their keel grated upon the pebbly bottom of the cove, they could see Rusty, the puppy, scampering along the beach to greet them. Ping was out of the boat in a moment. Rusty ran round him in circles, making little dives and bounces to lick his face and worry his feet, and at length Ping lifted him in his arms and carried him to the house.

The others followed more slowly. When they reached the house, they found letters on the hall table. There was one for Trudy from home and she ran upstairs quickly to read it. Nancy ran after her.

"Hi! Don't keep all the news to yourself!"

There was very little news. Just that their parents were both well, though missing their family. Mum was a bit worried because Abednego, Ping's cat, had been out all night and hadn't yet returned.

"However, I have no doubt he will put in an

appearance soon. In any case, don't say a word
to Ping."

"If his cat's lost, Ping will never get over it,"
observed Nancy.

"Oh, he'll turn up all right," Trudy assured her.

For the moment, Ping seemed to have forgotten
about his cat and was having a merry time with
Rusty on the lawn.

Most of the guests again repaired to the Silver
Beach in the afternoon. This time, Mrs. Cooper
joined them. Trudy walked with her across the
field, but she found her a very silent companion.
She had the air of not listening to what was said
and her face never once relaxed in a smile. She
probably thinks that as I'm only a schoolgirl, I'm
not worth talking to, thought Trudy. She wished
she were a bit older and wiser to know how to break
down her companion's reserve; but if her own
husband found it impossible, what chance had she?

Eva and her grandmother were at the beach
when they arrived, the old lady sitting on a bench
knitting a stocking, while Eva played in the sand
some distance away. Ping went down to join her,
and Trudy and Nancy went to a secluded sand
quarry to get ready for their bathe. The water
was cold at first, but they soon got used to it.
Nancy swam out expertly, but Trudy was content
to remain in the shallows practising a few amateur
strokes.

After dressing, she sat down to read, near where
Ping and Eva were playing. But the sea had made
her drowsy and she felt herself dozing over to the
accompaniment of the voices of the children, who
were building a house in the sand.

CHAPTER V

At Rocky Point

"IT'S a funny kind of house," Eva was saying dubiously. "It's got a flat sort of roof. And where are the windows?"

"Wait and see," was Ping's brusque reply. "This isn't an ordinary house. It's special, like the houses in Palestine."

"Where's Palestine?"

Ping wasn't sure himself, but he was seldom at a loss. "Away over there—" he pointed towards the sea. "In the East, where the wise men came from."

"What wise men?"

"The ones in the Bible. There were three of them. They followed a bright star in the sky and it took them to the manger where the baby Jesus was. Don't you go to Sunday School at all?"

Eva shook her head. "Grandma won't let me. Tell me more, Ping, about Jesus."

"Well," continued the boy, "when He grew to be a man, He did miracles and He was very kind and good, and He told people about God."

"What's miracles?" asked the persistent little girl.

"You don't know much, do you?" He patted his sand-house scornfully. "Miracles are wonderful things that folk like you and me couldn't do, like making the sea be calm, and changing water into wine, and making sick people well again. Jesus could do all these."

As she listened, Trudy smiled to herself. Assuredly, Ping would make an excellent preacher some day. His present audience was hanging on his words.

"Tell me a miracle, Ping!"

"Well," he began, "do you see this sand-house? Jesus was in a house like this one day, speaking to people and curing those that were ill. There was such a crush, lots of folk had to go away without seeing Him. Then along came four men carrying a stretcher and on it was a man so ill he couldn't walk. They couldn't manage to get into the house by the door, and do you know what they did?"

"No. Please tell me!"

"They went up on the roof and made a hole in it, and lowered the stretcher down, right in front of Jesus."

"And did He make the man well?" gasped Eva.

"Sure, He did. He said to the man, 'Arise and take up thy bed and walk—' and the man got up and walked, just as though he'd never been ill. You see, he believed that Jesus could cure him. That's what you call faith."

Eva regarded him solemnly.

"Tell me some more," she demanded.

Ping took her at her word, and the Bible stories were still being told when tea-time came around.

When they got back to the house, the Lawsons found that David's chair at the table was empty.

"I wonder where David has got to?" Though she was younger than her brother, Trudy still felt responsible for him.

"He was going to walk to Rocky Point," said Ping, "to finish his picture."

"It must be dangerous walking round there,

with all those slippery rocks and cliffs."

"I wanted to go with him, but he wouldn't let me," complained Ping.

"I do hope he takes care. If he happened to sprain his ankle or anything, there would be no one to help."

"Stop fussing, True." Nancy was doing justice to the sandwiches. "David's not a baby."

"All the same, if he doesn't come soon, I'm going to look for him. You, too, Nancy?"

Her sister shook her head. "I'm going to help Miss Stewart make supper. Peggy, the maid, has gone to bed with a cold."

"Dear me, you seem to have gone all domestic."

Nancy flushed. "Miss Stewart's got an awful lot to do. Why shouldn't I help her?"

"No reason at all."

"I hope you don't start breaking dishes the way you do at home," observed Ping.

Trudy laughed. "I think we should warn Miss Stewart what to expect."

Nancy got up from the table indignantly.

"I think you're mean! Making fun of me when I'm trying to do a good turn," and she marched out of the room.

Trudy had only been teasing, but she felt slightly conscience-stricken.

"Never mind her, True. I'll come with you to look for David, may I?"

"I suppose so," she told Ping as, having finished tea, they prepared to leave the table.

She went straight up to the bedroom, but Nnacy was not there. The two sisters seldom quarrelled, for their mother seemed to have the knack of smoothing things over at the first signs of difference, but sometimes Nancy was inclined to take offence at very little.

Hoping that she would soon forget her annoyance, wherever she had got to, Trudy put on a pair of stout walking shoes and her raincoat, for there were heavy clouds on the horizon. Ping was waiting for her in the backyard, where Mr. Stewart was busy splitting firewood. Trudy smiled and said "good afternoon."

The big, grim-looking man returned the greeting without the smile.

"We were thinking of walking round to Rocky Point, Mr. Stewart. Is it quite safe?"

"Quite safe, if you're careful," he replied. "But it's heavy going. Keep well up among the dry rocks and don't try to climb those that have seaweed on them. You'd be better with a stick. Bide there a minute."

He disappeared inside the shed, to return with a couple of stout sticks cut from a tree.

They set off across the field and were just reaching the shore, when an excited barking sounded behind them and they turned to see Rusty scampering after them. He jumped up on Ping, licking his face joyfully.

"Home, Rusty, home!" commanded Trudy. But Rusty was not taking any orders. He was only a pup and had not yet learned to obey.

"Let him come, Trudy! He'll be all right."

There seemed nothing else to do but to allow Rusty to accompany them. At first the going was easy. There was soft turf and bracken for them to walk on, and the rocks were far enough apart to allow them to scramble through. Soon, however, the turf became broken and water-logged, with big holes in it which they had to jump across. It was here that the sticks became useful.

Everything was very still, almost eerie. They heard strange bird-calls and every now and then a gull with a raucous cry would dive into the water to catch a fish.

And still there was no sign of David.

"Perhaps he didn't come this way, after all," suggested Ping.

Their pace slackened a bit, only Rusty racing on with unabated vigour. He examined every rabbit hole and darted here and there after imaginary prey. Then the way became really difficult, for they had to scale high rocks. At the top of one of these, Trudy's foot suddenly slipped and she found herself falling down the rough slope. It was not very far, but her hands were cut and bleeding, and when she rose to her feet she felt quite shaky. Ping was alarmed.

"Oh, Trudy, are you killed?"

"Not yet," she assured him. "But I don't feel like going any further. Let's go back, Ping."

"But True, we don't need to. We're nearly there!"

He pointed and there, sure enough, was the long, jagged peninsula called Rocky Point. What was more, seated a few yards away, oblivious to everything but the scene he was painting, was the brother they had come to seek.

Ping plunged forward joyfully, while Trudy limped behind. She felt quite angry with David, bringing them all this way.

At Ping's shouts, he looked up.

"Whatever brought you two here?"

"David, it must be almost supper-time! We

wondered what had happened to you!"

He passed his hand across his eyes, as if to bring himself back to earth.

"I didn't know it was so late. I just went on painting without bothering about the time."

Trudy could well believe it. When David was painting, he always forgot everthing else. Then she looked over his shoulder at the water-colour on his easel and all her irritation fled.

"David! It's good! It's the best thing you've ever done!"

He had painted the long, jagged line of rocks with the foam breaking on them. Above was a turquoise sky with a bunch of rain-clouds on the horizon, and in the foreground was the flat beach, interspersed with rocks and pools. The picture was as vivid as the scene itself, and for the first time Trudy realized that this brother of hers had the makings of a very talented artist.

"It's not bad," murmured David, modestly. "Not quite what I wanted, but I agree it's the best thing I've done yet. If only I could get another half-hour! But the light's going."

As he spoke, a spot of rain fell on his hand and he covered his picture quickly.

"That settles it. We'll have to get home."

They called on Ping, who had disappeared with the pup in the direction of the cave, and he came running towards them with pink cheeks and shining eyes.

"What do you think? The convict's been here!"

David laughed disbelievingly. "There's been no convict around here or I should have seen him."

"He's gone now, but he slept in the cave, and he lit a fire. Look!"

He pointed to the fireplace at the mouth of the cave. It contained half-burned pieces of firewood which had not been there yesterday. Inside the cave there was a big heap of bracken flattened down, as if it had been slept on. Rusty was running round in circles sniffing at the ground.

"Yes, somebody has been here," agreed David. "A tramp, most likely. It's quite a cosy place to sleep in summer."

"I hope he's gone for good, then," Trudy remarked. "I shouldn't like to meet a tramp in such a lonely place."

"Or an escaped convict," supplied Ping, who had visions of himself bringing food and raiment to the poor, hunted man. All the way home he was laying plans to come back here by himself and meet the convict. He would be a nice, kind convict, of course, not a desperate one.

When they got back, after a hasty scramble across the rocks, none of them were fit to be seen. They were soaked with rain; Trudy's hands and knees were stained and cut, and Ping's were almost as bad. It took them all their time to get cleaned up for supper.

As they approached the dining room, Miss Stewart said to Trudy:

"I hope you don't mind, Miss Trudy, but your sister is very anxious to help me serve the meal. Will it be all right?"

"Yes, of course. I hope she's not in your way, Miss Stewart."

"Not at all. She's been a great help. It's not every girl would do it."

"What's all this?" muttered David, as they sat

at table. "I don't like the idea of Nancy attending the tables."

"There's nothing to be ashamed of in lending a helping hand," Trudy reminded him.

"Jesus washed the disciples' feet," put in Ping, unexpectedly. David flushed and held his tongue. When Nancy rather shyly came round with the cold meat and salad, Trudy gave her an encouraging smile:

"Bravo, Nancy. I'm sorry I made fun of you at tea-time."

"That's all right." She smiled forgivingly. "It's me that's far too touchy. I hope you like the salad I made."

"You made it? We'd better look out for caterpillars," retorted David, but for once Nancy did not take offence.

As usual, Eva at the window table showed more interest in Ping than she did in her food, and they could hear her grandmother speaking sharply to her. Miss Winton and Mr. Cooper both smiled at Nancy when she reached their table, but Mrs. Cooper's expressionless face did not relax. When supper was over, Trudy lent a hand also to clear the tables and she was last out of the dining room. There was a voice at her elbow:

"I've been waiting to speak to you alone, Miss Trudy Lawson."

It was Eva's grandmother. What fault had she to find now?

"It's about your young brother. He and my grand-daughter were playing together this afternoon."

"Yes, Mrs. Somers, I know that. Have you any objection? Ping is quite a harmless little boy, you know."

"I'm not so sure about that. Yesterday he encouraged Eva to go into the water. It's a wonder she did not get a chill. To-day, he seems to have been filling her head with a lot of religious nonsense."

Trudy's face flushed at her tone.

"I heard him, Mrs. Somers. But it wasn't 'religious nonsense,' as you call it. He was talking about Jesus and telling her about some of His miracles."

"They are both far too young to be bothering about religion," declared the other. "There's plenty of time to think about that when they are older."

"But their need of religion won't wait till they're older."

"You're wrong, my girl. I have reached a good age myself and I've never felt the need of religion yet."

Trudy was not quite sure what to reply. She hardly believed that what Mrs. Somers said was true. Though she was only fifteen, there had already been times in her life when she would have been utterly at a loss without the God her mother had taught her to believe in.

"Perhaps," she suggested, "you might come to need it yet, Mrs. Somers."

The only answer was a disbelieving laugh. Then she went on:

"You will please tell your brother never to speak to Eva about this 'Jesus' of his."

But Trudy was not going to submit to this. "Sorry, but I can't promise to do that. Ping is used to thinking and speaking about Jesus, because he loves Him just like a friend. He admires

Him and wants to be like Him. And so do I," she continued bravely.

"Indeed. And what exactly do you mean by that?" sneered her companion.

"Well," Trudy went on, "He was unselfish and pure in heart and He didn't care about money or possessions. He went about doing good, and He died for our sins that we might be forgiven. He is my Saviour. Of course, I could never be quite like Him; no one could. It's the trying that counts, and everyone can try," she continued earnestly.

Mrs. Somers looked at her perplexedly.

"You amaze me. I was under the impression that you modern girls were all out for a good time."

"Oh, no, Mrs. Somers. We like to have fun, of course, but that doesn't keep us from thinking about serious things as well. That is, quite a lot of us." Her mind went back to her chum Esther and some of the other girls at school who really tried to live up to the teaching of Jesus Christ.

At this point, Ping came running up to her with Rusty at his heels.

"Trudy, I've been waiting for you! Have you forgotten about my bedtime?"

"All right, Ping." She took her brother's grubby little hand in hers. "I'll have to go, Mrs. Somers. Good-night!"

"Good-night," said the other, shortly. But she stood at the door for a long time after they had gone, and the look on her proud face was strangely thoughtful.

CHAPTER VI

David's Picture

WHEN Trudy and Ping reached the tent, followed by Rusty, they found David standing there, hands in pockets, whistling moodily. His mind was still on his picture, and until he got it finished he would not be able to think of anything else. Ping was extra tired to-night with his scramble over the rocks, and he snuggled gratefully between the army blankets. Rusty settled down at his feet as if for the night.

"Sleeping in a tent's good fun, but I think a cave would be even better," sighed Ping.

"Give me a tent any day," declared Trudy. "There's too many creepy-crawly things about a cave." She stayed beside Ping while he said his prayers. He went over the list of the people in the house, putting in a special plea for Miss Winton.

"Please God, she has no father nor mother, and no little boys and no husband, and she is very lonely and sad because she can't sing any more. Bless her, dear God, and make her happy, and bless my convict that lives in the cave. If he's a good convict, make him escape and get back home, and if he's a wicked convict, please make him good."

Trudy kissed him good-night, laughing.

"He's probably not a convict at all, Ping."

"Well, anyhow, it does no harm to ask God to bless him."

"You're quite right, Ping. Good-night, then. Shall I ask David to stay beside you?"

But Ping did not want anyone to stay. He had Rusty, hadn't he?

As Trudy left the tent she saw David's picture in the corner, and took it outside with her.

"David, may I take this to show Mrs. Stewart? I'm sure she would love it."

"All right, I don't mind. I'll walk to the house with you, Trudy."

On the way they met Mr. Cooper going for a stroll alone.

"Where is his wife?" David asked when he had passed. "Why does she never go out with him?"

Trudy tried to explain: "They lost their little girl. Mrs. Cooper doesn't seem able to forget. And because her husband wants to do the things they used to do, she gets cross with him. I'm so sorry for them both, aren't you?"

"I daresay. But there's nothing we can do about it," said David.

"If only there was. I often think that if I were a bit older I could help people more. But people seem to think girls of my age don't know anything," replied Trudy.

"The older you get, the more you realize how little you know."

Trudy puzzled this out. It might be true, as far as worldly wisdom went, but there were other kinds of wisdom. Hadn't Jesus said: 'Unless ye become as little children'?

When they reached the house, Trudy asked David if he would not like to come in and see Mrs. Stewart.

"But she's an invalid, isn't she? I never know what to say to people who are ill."

"Never mind about that. She doesn't give the impression of being ill. She knows Brian Clyde, David. He comes to see her sometimes."

This piece of news won David over.

Trudy knocked at Mrs. Stewart's door, and they both entered. The sweet perfume of honeysuckle greeted them, and the room was bathed in the soft light of the setting sun.

To-night, the invalid's grey shawl had been replaced by a filmy bed jacket of shell-pink, and there was a narrow pink ribbon through her snow-white hair.

"Look at me, all dressed up like a dish of fish! Your sister Nancy has just been in decking me up. How do you like me?"

"Very much." Trudy thought how pretty she must have been when a girl. To-day, her beauty was of a different kind. It had been refined by experience, and Trudy realized that true beauty is a thing that never fades.

She introduced David. "We've brought his painting to show you."

Mrs. Stewart glanced with interest from David to the vivid water-colour of rock and sea.

"It's very fine indeed. I know that scene well. I used to love to go there. Many a cut knee I've got on these same rocks. It brings back a lot of memories." It seemed that she could not look long enough.

"It's not quite finished yet," David told her. "I'll be putting on the finishing touches to-morrow. Would you like to have the picture to hang in your room, Mrs. Stewart?"

Trudy was surprised at the offer. She had thought David would want to keep what was his best work up till now.

"Do you mean it, laddie? I'd be very grateful indeed."

"All right," said David. "You shall have it to-morrow."

He stayed for a few minutes before taking his leave. After he had gone, Mrs. Stewart said to Trudy:

"David is a fine lad. You two girls must be proud of him."

"Well, not really. We tease him a lot. He used to be a very moody boy, but he's improving."

"You wait. He's going to surprise you one day. That's an excellent picture; and how kind of him to give it to me! Everyone is kind to me. That's one of the benefits of being ill. You find out how much good there is in people."

"As if anyone would be anything but good to you!" Trudy sat down beside the bed. "Would you like me to read to you to-night?"

"Yes, dear. I would very much like to hear the 42nd Psalm."

As she was turning up the chapter, there was a knock at the door, and Miss Winton looked in to ask: "How are you to-night, Mrs. Stewart?"

"Very well, thank you. Come right in. Trudy is just going to read me a Psalm."

The newcomer looked embarrassed. "Perhaps I'd better come back some other time."

"Please do come in," pleaded Trudy.

She complied slowly, and took a seat by the window which looked out to the field where the boys' tent was. Studying her profile, Trudy observed the sad droop of her head and the bitter line of her mouth. How sorely she had taken to heart the loss of her voice and all her prospects in life!

It would need something very big and wonderful to restore her to happiness. Many would have said it was impossible, but Trudy knew better, and so did Mrs. Stewart.

Trudy read slowly, giving to each phrase its full, poetic meaning.

"As the hart panteth after the water-brooks, so panteth my heart after Thee, O God."

The words fell on Olivia Winton's ears with a strange sweetness.

"My tears have been my meat day and night, while they continuously say unto me, Where is thy God?"

How often had she asked herself that question!

Trudy read on: "Why art thou cast down, O my soul? And why art thou disquieted within me? Hope thou in God for I shall yet praise Him for the help of His countenance."

When she had finished, she closed the Bible and Mrs. Stewart put it back under her pillow.

"Thank you, Trudy. It is good to hear those beautiful words read in your clear, young voice."

"I love the Psalms," said Trudy.

"They are very musical," murmured Olivia. "I wish—" she stopped, with a sigh.

"Yes, my dear?" Mrs. Stewart waited for an answer, but none came. "Wouldn't you like to speak out all that is in your mind?"

Olivia shook her head. But she rose and came over to take the frail hand in hers. "Someday you and I will have another talk. But I can't think clearly yet. I feel too hopeless."

"Let it be soon," said the other. "I'll be praying for you."

When Trudy and Olivia left the room, the latter

said: "Are you doing anything special to-morrow forenoon, Trudy? I thought we might go for a walk together, but I'm rather dull company, I'm afraid."

"No, you are not," Trudy told her. "May I bring Nancy too?"

"Of course. I suppose the boys will have their own plans?"

"Yes. David wants to finish his picture, and Ping will be going with him to see his cave. He's quite sure an escaped convict slept there last night."

Upstairs in the bedroom, she found Nancy fast asleep in the middle of the bed as usual. She lit the candle and sat down to write a few lines to her mother. What a lot seemed to have happened since morning! They had been to Waterside in the boat, had heard the fishermen singing and had seen Brian Clyde. At the Silver Beach in the afternoon, Ping had told Eva about Jesus, and Mrs. Somers had been angry. Then, this evening, Ping and she had had an adventurous journey to Rocky Point. David had nearly finished his picture and had promised to give it to Mrs. Stewart.

"I think it is very generous of David," she wrote. "My opinion of him has gone up with a bound." On and on she wrote, till her fountain pen went dry. To her mother she always expressed everything that was in her heart. Sometimes it was easier to do this by writing than by talking. Trudy was one of these people who find it easier to think with a pen in hand. Her letters always made good reading, for she did not attempt to write fine, stylish language, but put down her thoughts in the simplest terms. Sometimes she wrote verses, and she kept a notebook with some of her poems in it, which she hoped to add to during the holiday.

She finished her letter by expressing the hope that Abednego had turned up safely, and sent their combined love to both at home. Having come to an end, she was only too glad to creep in beside Nancy and lose herself in sleep.

Next morning she was awakened by the voice of Nancy in her ear:

"I'm glad we came here for a holiday. Now I know what I'm going to be when I grow up."

"What's that?" asked Trudy sleepily.

"A nurse. I loved attending to Mrs. Stewart last night. I helped her to wash, and brushed her hair and put a ribbon in it."

"Yes, I thought she looked very sweet. But being a nurse is more than just dressing people up. It's very hard work."

"But if you're doing work you like, you don't find it hard."

Trudy agreed that was the case. When she was writing a school essay, for instance, it did not seem like work. It all depended on what one's abilities and preferences were.

"Perhaps you'll change your mind," she told Nancy. "After all, you're only thirteen."

Nancy did not like to be reminded that she was two years younger than her sister.

"What about it? In some ways I know more than you do. I'm going to be a nurse, because I want to help people. I'd hate to be something that was only for myself."

Nancy was growing up. A few months ago, she would not have voiced such a thought. Trudy turned her head and smiled at her impulsive younger sister.

"You've got the right idea, kid. Oh, dear, there's the getting-up bell! By the way, have you any objection to coming for a walk with Miss Winton and me this morning?"

"Not very exhilarating company, is she?"

"Neither would you be, if all your hopes had been dashed." She rolled out of bed and began to put on her clothes. "Let's try to exhilarate her, Nancy."

Nancy promised to do her best. Later, while she and Trudy were waiting on the lawn for Miss Winton, they saw Mr. Cooper coming out of the house with his golf-bag on his shoulder. He stopped to speak, and they told him they were going for a walk.

"Perhaps you could ask my wife to go with you?" he asked eagerly. "She doesn't want to come on the golf-course and I'm afraid she might be lonely."

Trudy said she would run up to her room and ask her, but as Mr. Cooper walked away, Nancy groaned.

"More aged females! It's not going to be a very cheerful forenoon."

"If you're going to be a nurse," Trudy told her, "you'll have to do worse things than take your elders for a walk. Besides, Miss Winton's not aged. I'm sure she'll only be about twenty-five or so."

"Twenty-five is aged," maintained Nancy, as Trudy ran off to see Mrs. Cooper. She did not exactly relish the prospect, for since their arrival the lady had not given them one friendly look.

Knocking at her bedroom door and hearing a muffled voice bidding her enter, she turned the handle. Mrs. Cooper was standing at the dressing-table in a defensive attitude. Her eyes were red, and Trudy was sure she had been weeping.

"What do you want?" she enquired.

"Nancy and I are going for a walk with Miss Winton, and Mr. Cooper suggested that you might want to come too."

"Mr. Cooper was wrong, I'm afraid. I prefer to stay in my room," was the cool reply.

That ought to have been enough, but Trudy remembered her resolution to try to make friends, and went on:

"It's a lovely day, Mrs. Cooper. Don't you think it would do you good?"

"I don't need a girl like you to tell me what's good for me. It's kind of you to ask me, but I don't wish to go."

There was no more to be said, so Trudy closed the door and went downstairs. "A girl like you—" Why did so many grown-ups persist in thinking that young folk were not worth listening to? It was very discouraging, to say the least. Trudy determined that when she herself got on in years, she would keep an open mind and remember that youth often has worthwhile things to say and has a right to be heard.

Miss Winton had joined Nancy on the lawn, and the three of them started to walk in the direction of Silver Beach.

"I believe you can get right round to Waterside this way," said Miss Winton, "but there are stepping-stones to cross."

They walked on across the firm, smooth sand on which the shallow water rippled in little foaming waves. Nancy took off her shoes and ran along with her pig-tails bobbing behind her, while the other two journeyed more soberly, Miss Winton telling Trudy more about herself, and her old uncle, who was the only relation she had in the world.

By and by they sat down to rest on a bank of turf, studying the beauty around them. The Waterside fishing-boats were clustered at the mouth of the river and behind them the island peaks rose to the sky. All about them wild flowers were blossoming: sea-pinks, fragrant myrtle, daisies and clover. From a handful of sand Trudy picked a beautiful shell, so delicate that a tap from her finger would shatter it. A verse of the Bible flashed into her mind: 'The heavens declare the glory of God; and the firmament showeth His handiwork.'

And yet there were people who could look on a scene like this and not believe in God. How could they help but believe?

CHAPTER VII

The Stepping-Stones

THAT walk with Miss Winton and Nancy was one which Trudy was to remember all her life.

They resumed their journey towards the stepping-stones and Waterside, only to find that the tide was in and the river was fairly wide and deep. Looking at them from the bank, the stones seemed very far apart.

"Perhaps we ought to go back," said Miss Winton.

"No fears!" declared Nancy. "I'm going across. You two can follow if you like!" And, still in her bare feet, she sprang from one stone to another with a sureness and lightness that made the others smile.

"You can't expect an old person like me to do that!" exclaimed Olivia. "You'd better go before me, Trudy, and perhaps by then I'll have found courage."

"All right. If you're sure you don't mind—" and Trudy jumped across to the first stone, wavered a moment, then took the others with almost as much assurance as Nancy. From the other side she called to Olivia:

"Come on! It's not so bad as it looks!"

After some deliberation, Miss Winton stepped onto the first stone, then, more shakily, across to the second. With some hesitation she at last managed the third, which took her into mid-stream. There she stood for so long that Trudy asked: "Is something the matter?"

There was no need to ask, however. As Olivia stood there insecurely in the midst of the swirling water, her face was white and strained, and there was a look of fear on it.

"I can't, Trudy. I can't come any further!"

"Perhaps you'd better go back, then."

"No, I can't go back either. I'm afraid. Terribly afraid!"

It was plain to see that the nervous strain she had suffered during her illness was upon her again, and Trudy was afraid that in her panic she would fall into the river which had a strong current at that point. As she and Nancy stood helpless, they heard a voice behind them.

"It's all right, folk, don't worry!"

Out of the trees a man had stepped. They recognized the figure of Brian Clyde. In his khaki shorts and open-necked shirt he looked so brown and strong that the girls instantly felt he was capable of handling the situation.

"Keep quite still!" he called to Miss Winton. "I'm coming to help you."

In a second his shoes were off and he was buckling up his shorts.

"You've got a stick? Good!" Taking Trudy's stick to steady himself, he waded into the swirling current. Unfalteringly he stepped until he reached Miss Winton's side. Standing beside her he seemed as secure as a rock grounded in the stream.

"Put your hand on my shoulder," he said.

The feel of it under her trembling fingers was firm and reassuring.

"Here is the stick. Now, do you think you can reach the next stone?"

"I'll try," she said.

With one hand on his shoulder and the stick in the other, it seemed perfectly easy, and she had no difficulty reaching the other side. When her feet touched the opposite bank, she sank to the grass and covered her face with her hands. He stood looking at her compassionately.

"It's all right. It's over now," he said in a low voice.

She glanced up, her eyes searching the strong, kindly face above her.

"Thank you. It was silly of me to be afraid. But I have been ill and I haven't quite recovered."

He smiled reassuringly.

"You will be better soon."

His very voice had a quality that seemed to give her strength. He held out his hand and she got to her feet. Trudy looked on wonderingly. She had never met anyone before like this Brian Clyde.

"You had better come up to my house, all three of you. I think a cup of tea is indicated. I live up there." He pointed to the white house with the verandah.

"You are a friend of Mrs. Stewart's, aren't you?" asked Trudy. "We are staying at her house for a holiday."

Olivia, in a voice that was still weak, but with the colour coming back into her cheeks, made the introductions.

"Trudy and Nancy are sisters, and my name is Olivia Winton."

"Olivia Winton?" he said eagerly. "I was sure I had seen you somewhere before. I heard you

singing at a Forces' concert once, in Palestine.
I was in the Air Force, then. You have a glorious
voice, Miss Winton."

Trudy, walking beside her, could see the distress
on her face and she pressed her arm sympathetically.

"I don't sing now," said Olivia bravely. "I
don't suppose I'll ever sing again. It was my
illness."

For a moment he did not speak; then, in a tone
of deep regret, he murmured:

"I am sorry. I understand how you must feel."

They walked on in silence to the house. Seeing it
for the first time yesterday, they had little thought
to visit it so soon. On the verandah outside, some
people were reclining on camp chairs. They
looked pale and ill, but smiled a greeting as they
passed.

Brian Clyde took them into a room which had
a settee bed, a table and chairs, and a cupboard
with dishes.

"This is where I dine and sleep," he said. "Just
a moment, please, till I put on the kettle."

Lighting a small spirit stove, he set a tin kettle
upon it. Everything in the room was of the
simplest, and yet, surely he must be a rich man?

"I only use the one room in the house," he
explained. "My studio is outside. These people
you saw on the verandah are my guests. They have
been ill and can't afford to go for holidays, so they
help me to use my house."

Trudy thought it was a splendid idea, indicating
what a fine, unselfish character the man had.

Nancy asked to be allowed to put out cups.

"If you like, but I'm afraid there's only one
saucer!"

"And what do your guests do?" enquired Nancy.

He told them that there was a pantry and kitchen for their use and that each person looked after himself as far as possible.

From the moment they entered the room, Trudy had been attracted by a picture hanging on the wall. It was a painting of Jesus and His disciples. The eleven were seated on the floor in Eastern fashion, disturbed in the midst of a meal by the presence of their risen Lord. The gracious Figure standing there was speaking words of grave command: 'Go ye into all the world and preach the Gospel.' No ordinary artist had painted this picture. It had come from the brush of one who was both talented and full of faith in his subject. She had no doubt that Brian Clyde was the painter, and looked at him with a new respect.

After making some tea, he took a tin of biscuits from the cupboard and asked them to help themselves, as it was time for him to go down to the beach for his morning service.

"We had the pleasure of listening to your service yesterday," said Olivia.

His face lit up. "Five people in a boat? I saw you. Please come down when you are finished. We are always very pleased to see visitors," and with that he left them to themselves.

They drank the tea gratefully, and Trudy asked Olivia how she was feeling.

"Much better, thanks. I'm afraid I lost my nerve on those stepping-stones."

She was still aware of the sense of relief and absolute assurance that had come to her when she put her hand on Brian Clyde's shoulder. Here was a strong man, a good man; one who was like a 'rock in a weary land' to lost and wandering souls.

The service to-day followed the same pattern as yesterday. Hearing the singing from the house, they went down to the beach to stand on the fringe of the group of fishermen, some of whose wives and children were also present. After a short prayer, Brian Clyde talked to them on the subject of his picture: 'Go ye into all the world and preach the Gospel.'

True Christians should treat the Word of God and the message of salvation as something to be shared with others, he said. There was only one way to bring hope to the present world of strife, and that was to broadcast Christ's Gospel of peace and goodwill.

The simple talk reflected a lot of what Trudy herself had been thinking. She realized that even she, in her own small way, could help to spread the wonderful message. She could not preach, but she could go on voicing her convictions, even though, as in the case of Mrs. Somers, little attention was paid to them.

It was just like planting a seed. It might not seem to take root, but there was always the hope that one day life would spring from it.

After the service, Brian Clyde escorted them back to the stepping-stones where he said good-bye.

"I do hope you will come again."

They promised they would.

"I won't even try to thank you," said Olivia earnestly.

"There is no need," he replied, adding: "Will you tell Mrs. Stewart I am coming to see her soon?"

Returning over the sands, the two girls chatted incessantly, but Olivia Winton was deep in thought.

Mrs. Stewart, Trudy, Brian Clyde; these three people were strong in a faith she did not share. But her attitude was changing. Whereas she had once thought that religion held nothing for her, she now began to wonder if it might not provide her with a strength and a purpose which she had been sorely lacking.

As they crossed the field, they met David and Ping coming from the opposite direction. Nancy was bursting to tell their news.

"We met Brian Clyde! We were in his house!"

David was disbelieving.

"It's true," Trudy assured him.

Though he pretended he didn't care, David would have given a lot for the chance of speaking to his hero. But he had done a good forenoon's work, and his painting was now complete.

Ping was excited, too. He had found fresh evidence of his 'convict'; a stack of firewood, an empty tin, and, most thrilling of all, footprints in the sand. But not a sign of the convict himself.

"I expect he hides during the day, but some day I'll find him."

"Well, I hope you're not disappointed if you do," said Nancy. "He'll probably just be a camper or a ragged old tramp."

But Ping preferred his own version of the mystery man. The subject was dropped when they saw Rusty scampering towards them and the sound of the luncheon gong made the party break into a run.

As they took their place at table, Trudy's eyes met Miss Winton's. Her cheeks were pink, and there was a sparkle about her that had been lacking before. Mr. Cooper was smiling across at them, too, but his wife's eyes were on her plate.

Then Eva slid off her chair and came over to say to Ping: "Are you going to the Silver Beach this afternoon?"

"Sure," was the reply. "I've got a great idea for a big sand tunnel."

"And will you tell me stories about Jesus, Ping?"

Ping did not get time to answer.

"Eva!" exclaimed Mrs. Somers. "Don't you know it is rude to leave the table like that? Come back at once." Then, "You've got no socks on! Where are they?"

"Upstairs," was the reply. "I don't want to wear socks any more, Grandma. Ping doesn't wear them, and neither do Nancy and Trudy. I'd like to have sandals, please, and a print frock like Nancy's."

Her grandmother was horrified.

"Such nonsense! Don't let me hear of it again. And you will put socks on immediately after lunch."

Eva heaved a sigh which made the Lawsons feel very sorry for her.

After the meal, they found Mr. Cooper studying David's picture which had been left in the hall.

"Remarkable! I must congratulate you, David. I had no idea we had such a talented artist in the house."

David flushed with pleasure.

"Oh, I'm just a beginner. I mean to do lots better than that some day, Mr. Cooper."

"It's really very mature for your age. You have an eye for colour." He turned to his wife. "It's a fine piece of work, isn't it, Agnes?"

"Yes, it certainly is." But the flicker of interest in his wife's eyes soon died away.

"In fact," went on Mr. Cooper, "I'd like to buy your picture, if you'd care to sell it, David. Will you accept a couple of guineas?"

It was quite a sum to a young fellow who had little or no pocket money. As he hesitated, Trudy wondered if he had forgotten about his promise to Mrs. Stewart.

"Perhaps I should make it three guineas. Who knows, some day you will be so famous I'll be able to sell it for a hundred!"

David was very pale now. The temptation was great, but he thrust it away from him.

"I'm sorry, Mr. Cooper, but the picture isn't for sale. You see, I promised to give it to Mrs. Stewart."

Trudy drew a breath of relief. Bravo, David!

"That's all right, my boy." Mr. Cooper laid a kindly hand on his shoulder. "A promise is a promise."

When they were left together, "Three guineas!" breathed Nancy. "Imagine missing all that money. Perhaps if you explain to Mrs. Stewart—"

"No," said Trudy, "David did the right thing. I'm proud of him. Would you like to come and give the picture to Mrs. Stewart now, David?"

"Take it in yourself, True. I hate 'thank-yous' and all that sort of thing."

David escaped outside and walked towards the tent. Though he was glad he had refused Mr. Cooper's offer, he could not help speculating on the 'publicity' he might have got from accepting it. No-one was ever likely to see his picture now. Oh, well, if it gave pleasure to a lonely invalid, it wasn't quite wasted. Money and fame weren't the only things that mattered.

CHAPTER VIII

At Dunglas Bay

WITH David's picture in her hand, Trudy went straight into Mrs. Stewart's room and presented it to her. The old lady was very touched.

"I think there should be a frame somewhere to fit it, Trudy. Could you find my husband and ask him to get it?"

In the garden she managed to intercept Mr. Stewart as he set off for his work in the fields, and she made her request. He pointed to a shed near the house.

"Look in there, Missie." He never wasted any words. What a strong, dour type of man he was, she thought, the kind that would stick to his own opinion through thick and thin. Poor Donald Stewart; she could easily understand how his father's lack of sympathy had driven him from home.

Among the lumber in the shed, she soon found a narrow black frame that would do for the picture. Miss Stewart gave her a hammer and some tacks, and the job of framing it was soon accomplished as well as David could have done it himself.

Then she had the pleasure of hanging it on the wall alongside Donald's photograph where Mrs. Stewart would be able to see it as she lay. Promising to come back again at night, she left her, picking up from the hall table a letter which had

newly arrived from her mother. She took it upstairs to read, and there found Nancy in front of
the mirror, dabbing cold cream on her nose where
the skin had begun to peel.

"Look, Trudy, amn't I a sight? Some folk can
get sunburned and remain beautiful, but not me!"

"You weren't even beautiful to start with,"
was the withering retort. "Listen, here's a letter
from Mum," and she started to read it aloud.

Everything was very quiet at home, said her
mother. The next-door house was shut up, as
Mrs. Drysdale was away visiting her sister and her
son Stephen was on his honeymoon. Stephen
Drysdale, after recovering his sight, which he had
lost through an aeroplane accident, had married
Trudy's English teacher, Miss Forsyth. The girls
were excited about the romance, but it meant the
school was losing its favourite mistress.

"Oh, Nancy, listen to this. Poor Abednego
hasn't come back yet. They're afraid he's gone
for good. How are we going to tell Ping?"

"Don't tell him yet. He might come back.
Cats do."

Their mother's last paragraph ran: "We are so
glad you are enjoying Ardensheel. It is like you,
Trudy, to want to make other people as happy as
you are yourself. I do hope you succeed. It
looks as if your fellow guests, Miss Winton and Mrs.
Cooper, not to mention Mrs. Somers, have missed
the one true source of happiness and peace of mind.
Mrs. Stewart has got what these others lack. Perhaps she can help you to bring some light into their
darkness."

Trudy folded the letter back into its envelope.
By this time Nancy was packing their bathing

things into the beach bag, and they set off for the
Silver Beach shortly afterwards.

It was on the journey back, as they all straggled
across the fields, that Ping said suddenly:

"There's just one thing wrong with this place.
There's no ice-cream!"

Not even in the village did they cater for the
tastes of small boys.

"Dunglas Bay is the nearest place for ice-cream,
I suppose," said Trudy.

"Then may I go there to-morrow, me and Eva?"

"Not alone."

Ping's eager face registered disappointment.

Mr. Cooper laughed.

"Cheer up, Ping! I'll take you and Eva into
Dunglas Bay to-morrow. In fact, I'll take anyone
who cares to come. What about it, Trudy?
There are bathing boxes and tearooms and ice-
cream by the gallon."

Trudy and Nancy expressed their approval.

"Isn't there a pool with a diving-board and raft?"
asked Nancy.

"That's right. My wife bathed there last summer. She is a very fine swimmer. Perhaps she
will come too." Mrs. Cooper had stayed at home
this afternoon and his voice did not sound very
hopeful.

"I hope you are not including me in the invita-
tion," said Eva's grandmother, who was with them.
"I don't mind Eva going, because I feel you will be
responsible for her, Mr. Cooper, but diving-boards
and rafts don't appeal to me, and neither does ice-
cream." There was a kind of dry humour in her voice.

"May Eva come into the water, just to paddle?"
asked Ping.

"She didn't come to any harm the last time," put in Trudy.

"Please, Grandma!" asked the child. "Just for a teeny-weeny while?"

After some hesitation, Mrs. Somers gave a doubtful consent.

Was she softening? Trudy wondered.

They found Mrs. Cooper sitting on the garden seat with Miss Winton. Her husband went up and laid a hand on her shoulder.

"I'm taking the young folk to Dunglas Bay to-morrow. You too, Miss Winton, if you care to come. I hope you'll join us, Agnes?"

"There will be ice-cream," urged Ping. "Pailfuls of it."

When Mrs. Cooper murmured: "Well, perhaps," Trudy felt as if a victory had been won.

That evening after supper she sat in the bedroom writing to her mother:

"This is the end of our fourth day. Such a lot has happened since we came here, and yet a casual onlooker would say nothing had happened at all—certainly nothing that would find a place in the newspaper headlines! What goes on inside us is never reported in the news, but sometimes it is of far greater importance than more spectacular events. Miss Winton, for example—I'm sure a great change is working in her. Even Mrs. Somers isn't quite so hard as when we came. Mrs. Cooper is a problem, but she is coming with us to-morrow to Dunglas Bay and I am hoping great things from that."

When the letter was finished, she opened the notebook which she kept for her 'inspirations.' Since listening to Brian Clyde's address, she had

been longing to put down her thoughts in verse.
After many tries, she managed to compose the
following:

> I planted a seed in my garden;
>   The skies were cold and grey;
> I'd little hope that life would spring
>   From the seed I planted that day.
>
> But after weeks of waiting,
>   When hope had almost fled,
> There sprang a shoot, young, strong, and green,
>   From the seed that had seemed quite dead.
>
> It grew to a beautiful blossom,
>   A joy to all around;
> A flower that never would have bloomed
>   Had that seed not lain in the ground.
>
> So I'll plant the seeds of Christ's teaching,
>   For I know that along the way,
> There are empty hearts where these seeds will bloom
>   Like the one I planted that day.

When, quite late, she crept into bed, she felt
strengthened in her desire to go through life
planting her seeds, no matter how sterile the ground
or how hopeless the prospects.

Next day, there was a cheerful bustle in the house
as, after lunch, they got ready for their journey to
Dunglas Bay. They did not intend to be home
for tea, as Mr. Cooper had promise them all a meal
in a tea-room. The big beach bag was packed
again with the bathing things, and Trudy and
Nancy were the last to set off.

Mr. Stewart was in the garden as they passed.
He had just picked from the ground a rose which
had been broken off its bush. Trudy had noticed

this rose-bush before, for its flowers were of an unusual shade of salmony-pink, and their texture was like velvet. Though she was still rather afraid of this dour, elderly man, she smiled at him and said:

"What a lovely rose! It's a pity it's been broken."

"Ay." He looked from the flower to her bright, shining face. "You can have it if you like, to pin on your frock."

"Oh, thanks!" She took the flower gratefully, touching his big, hard hand with her light fingers: "It's kind of you."

When they joined the others. "Look what Mr. Stewart gave me!" she said.

"You must be a special favourite," teased Miss Winton. "I'm sure he's not in the habit of giving roses to young ladies."

Trudy was happy to think that Mr. Stewart must like her a little, in spite of his grim exterior.

They had not long to wait at the stop till the old red bus came trundling along. Eva sat beside Ping, with Trudy and David behind. Miss Winton and Nancy kept together, while the Coopers shared another seat. As they passed through the lovely scenery they had so admired on the first day, the tongues of the young folk wagged merrily. During a lull, Trudy could hear Ping humming to himself, as he often did when he was happy.

"What tune is that you're humming?" asked Eva.

"Oh, it's just a hymn we get in Sunday School."

"Sing it to me, Ping!"

In his sweet, piping voice, he sang the first verse:

If I come to Jesus, He will make me glad,
He will give me pleasure when my heart is sad.
If I come to Jesus, happy shall I be;
He is gently calling little ones like me.

"I like that," said Eva.   "I want to sing it too."

Ping was quite willing to teach her the hymn, and as the two young voices mingled sweetly together, the other occupants of the bus smiled in an amused but kindly fashion, and the eyes of more than one of them became dim, for nothing is more moving to the heart than the innocent voices of children singing some simple hymn.

Then Eva whispered in Ping's ear:

"Ping, could I come to Jesus?"

"Of course you could.   Everybody can, if they want to.   But lots of them don't."

"How could I come to Him?" she went on.

Ping thought a moment.   "You'd better ask Trudy," was his reply.

Eva glanced up at Trudy shyly, and Trudy smiled down at the pleading little face.

"You and I can have a talk about it to-night," she promised.

David had not much to say for himself to-day. Trudy thought it was a pity he had no companions here.

"Don't you wish you had a pal?" she asked.

"Well, if he was the right kind of pal."

"What would be the right kind?"

"Well, he'd have to be interested in painting and be a good sport, but not the kind to drag me round to places I didn't want to go; and he'd have to know when to leave me alone."

"You're a bit particular, aren't you?" she teased.

"I know.   I can't help it.   I'm not like you, Trudy.   You're one of the kind that can suffer fools gladly."

Trudy thought it useless to explain that some-times it took a great deal of effort to make oneself companionable. Perhaps girls were better at doing this than boys, but she hoped David would not always be so unsociable. He certainly was easier to get on with than he used to be, but he still had a lot to learn.

Now the bus was rattling into Dunglas Bay. Here was a scene totally different from the solitude of Ardensheel. The sands were busy with people and the sight of the shops gave them quite a thrill. There was a rush towards the ice-cream wagon on the beach, and as Ping's pink tongue at last travelled round a bulging ice-cream wafer, the look on his face was rapturous.

"I'm going to eat six before I go home!"

"And then you'll have a pain," said Nancy.

"Well, it will be worth it."

The girls made a bee-line for the bathing-boxes.

"Please, Mrs. Cooper, do come in to bathe," pleaded Nancy. "Mr. Cooper says you're an expert diver and I do want you to teach me."

"It's quite safe," Ping assured her. "There's no sharks or anything."

Trudy watched her face as she hesitated to reply. Then to her disappointment, Mrs. Cooper withdrew her arm from Nancy's.

"I'm sorry, but I don't feel like swimming to-day."

Nancy's sensitive face flushed over. Her lashes winked off a tear as she turned away. Trudy heard Mr. Cooper say to his wife:

"You've hurt that child's feelings, Agnes."

"Nonsense, Robert."

"It's a fact." He sighed. "You don't seem to mind about hurting folk these days. Perhaps if you thought of other people a little more—"

She turned on him angrily:

"I won't have you talking to me like that!" and she turned and left him, making her way to a bench on the grassy sward overlooking the bathers, where Miss Winton was already seated.

Trudy took refuge in a bathing-box, feeling sorry for them both. Mr. Cooper was such a decent sort, giving them this treat. Why didn't his wife appreciate him more?

While Ping and Eva played at the edge, the two girls, with David and Mr. Cooper, took the plunge into water which, though cold at the first impact, soon made them glow. Nancy could swim further than any of them, but Trudy had less confidence. As long as she had one toe on the ground, she was all right, but after one or two strokes, she always felt as if she was going to sink, and would splutter and swallow mouthfuls of salt water.

Nancy called to her to come out where it was deeper. "It's easier to swim here!"

She waded out almost to her shoulders and Nancy held her chin while she swam.

"Now, lie on your back and float."

With difficulty, Trudy turned round and tried to obey instructions, but with little success.

"I'll never make a swimmer," she sighed.

"Oh, well, you can't be good at everything," her sister comforted her.

Ping was laughing at her from the shallow water.

"You look like a dying duck in a thunderstorm!"

For answer, Trudy waded in and splashed him till he squealed. Eva was enjoying the fun.

"I'm going to ask my Gran for a bathing suit, too, as well as sandals and a cotton frock."

"No harm asking," said Ping, "but you'll not get it."

"Yes, I shall. If I keep on at her every minute, she'll say yes. Just wait and see."

Trudy foresaw trouble ahead. Her teeth were chattering now and she thought it best to go in. A rub-up with the rough towel she had brought restored her circulation. Then she dressed, not forgetting to pin her rose on her frock. Its perfume filled the small bathing-hut and went with her as she walked along the sand.

Little incidents sometimes lead to a turning of the ways in people's lives. If Trudy had left her rose behind her in the bathing-hut, after events would have been quite different, but she was not to know that at the time.

CHAPTER IX

The Man with the Red Beard

AFTER the bathers had dressed, Mr. Cooper organized a game of cricket on the sand. Miss Winton came down to join them, but Mrs. Cooper preferred to remain a spectator.

The three males agreed to play against the four females, though Nancy said it wasn't fair, men were so much better at games. It certainly seemed a poor look-out for their side when she and Trudy and Eva were dismissed for six runs, leaving Miss Winton in to bat.

It was evident that David did not expect much from such an opponent, for he bowled very softly and was astounded when Miss Winton sent the first ball swooping over the sand across their 'six' boundary. That sent the score up to twelve and David was more careful next time. Nevertheless, the score continued to mount, and it was not until the female side had made fifty-six that Mr. Cooper at last sent the ball crashing against the stumps and Miss Winton retired, laughing and breathless, with her side cheering madly.

"What a lovely surprise innings!" Nancy practically hugged her. "Where on earth did you learn to play cricket?"

"Various places. I was in the girls' team at school. But I'm not really much good at batting. It's bowling I like."

When the other side went in, they found it was

as much as they could do to deal with Miss Winton's rapid 'googlies.' Ping went out for a 'duck,' and Mr. Cooper was pronounced L.B.W. at fifteen.

Then David went in to make a fight for it. Trudy took the bowling to give Miss Winton a rest, but David knocked her balls here, there and everywhere. Nancy managed no better, and Eva's efforts only got halfway across the pitch. At fifty-five, when the girls had given up all hope, Miss Winton went in to bowl. As she took her stance, ball in hand, smiling mischievously at David, Nancy whispered to Trudy:

"I take back what I said about her age. She looks quite young just now, doesn't she? She might even get a husband one of these days."

"Hush," rebuked Trudy, as the ball left Miss Winton's hand, to trace a simple curve in the air. David lifted his bat to give it a disastrous whack, but it did not land where he expected, and he was obliged to ladle it up with a gentle lob, an easy catch for whoever was waiting for it.

Trudy saw it coming, and an excited lump rose to her throat. She was a coward about cricket balls; they were so hard! But Miss Winton had done her bit; she must do hers, too. Going forward warily, her eyes on the ball, she tensed herself for the catch. Here it was. Tring! Her palm was stinging, but the ball was in it, safe and sound.

"Goody! We've won!" Nancy and Eva leaped about gleefully, while their opponents groaned.

"Ugh," muttered Ping, "we didn't do our best. If we had, we could have beaten you easily."

"Not a bit of it!" Mr. Cooper shook hands with the victors. "They put up an excellent show.

Another day we'll have our revenge. Now, what about some tea?"

Mrs. Cooper joined them as they made for the cafe across the road.

"Did you enjoy watching the game?" Trudy asked her.

"It was quite interesting," was the listless reply.

Was it utterly impossible to surmount the barrier between them?

The company filled two tables. Mr. Cooper ordered tea, sandwiches and cakes, and they lost no time in doing justice to the meal.

Through the window they could see the steamer lying at the pier. She was due to leave for the mainland in about half an hour.

"I'm glad we're not going home yet," mumbled Ping, his mouth full of raisin bun. "I could stay here for ever, playing cricket and eating ice-cream, no school to go to, and the sun always shining. Wouldn't it be fun!"

"But we wouldn't enjoy it if we had it always," was Nancy's remark. "We've got to have dark days so that we can appreciate bright ones."

"Quite true, Nancy," said Mr. Cooper. "There's nothing wrong with your thinking apparatus, I see."

While they were eating, Trudy found her attention drawn to the occupant of another table whose eyes were upon her. He was dressed in a shabby tweed suit and wore a bushy red beard. She got the impression that she had seen him somewhere before, but decided that she was mistaken. Still, he was looking at her very keenly, though giving no sign of recognition.

She forgot about the man until it was time for

them to leave and they had to pass his table. Then she noticed that at his feet was a big leather suitcase pasted over with labels from foreign countries. Evidently he had travelled far, and was probably leaving the island with the steamer which now lay at the pier. Mr. Cooper had noticed him, too.

"Rather a strange apparition for these parts!" he remarked as they went outside.

"Excuse me," said a voice beside Trudy. "I found this rose in the cafe. I think it is yours."

The bearded stranger was standing there with her rose in his hand.

"Thank you so much," she said gratefully.

"It's quite an unusual colour. Would you mind telling me where it came from?"

"From Ardensheel," she told him. "From the Stewarts' garden."

His eyes were still on the rose in his hand. "I've only seen one rose bush like this in my life; the colour, so delicate, and the texture like velvet."

"Yes, it's very lovely." Then she added: "If you like it so much, I think you should keep it."

"You're quite sure? You would give your rose to a stranger?"

"Of course. I believe in sharing. Please keep it."

"Thank you," he said, a trifle huskily. "I'll accept it gladly."

There was an emotion in his voice which Trudy could not understand. Ping was staring at him with undisguised interest.

"Have you been to all these places?" He pointed to the labels on the suitcase, where he was spelling out the names—New York, Boston, Philadelphia.

"Sure I have, sonny."

"I wish I could travel. It must be fine to see all these grand towns."

"You'll never see anything grander than what's around you just now," was the reply, as he laid a brown hand on Ping's hair. "Young folk sometimes make the mistake of thinking that the best things are over the hill, but often they are just beside us. So take a good look, before you decide to go travelling, my lad." He thanked Trudy again, and with the rose in his lapel, he picked up his suitcase and went towards the pier.

"I like him," said Ping, "but his beard is a bit frightening."

"That's the kind of beard David is going to grow some day," ventured Nancy, "when he's a famous artist."

Her brother gave her hair an avenging tug: "It would look better than your pigtails, anyway!"

There was just time for Ping and Eva to buy some more ice-cream before their bus appeared, and they clambered aboard, unkempt but happy. On the way home, Trudy said to Miss Winton, who was sitting beside her:

"Have you had a good time?"

"Yes, I've enjoyed it. A few days ago I wouldn't have believed I could have been so light-hearted. You're a good pal, Trudy. Without you, I'd still have been in the depths."

Trudy was taken aback. "Oh, but I haven't done anything!"

"You have indeed. Some people act as a tonic to others. You've been a tonic to me, Trudy."

Her words made Trudy blush. And yet, if her company had been good for Miss Winton, it was no credit to her, but to the things she believed in.

She had heard of people speak of her mother as being 'as good as a tonic,' and could think of no worthier aim than trying to follow in her footsteps.

Mrs. Somers was waiting in the porch when they arrived back. Their merry voices were hushed when they saw the expression on her face.

"Eva, whatever have you been doing to yourself?"

This was a different Eva from the immaculate little girl of a few hours ago. Her hair had lost its ribbon and was tangled round her head, her silk frock looked bedraggled, her legs were bare and shoes no longer white. But there was a healthy glow on her face and her eyes were sparkling. Mrs. Somers took no account of this, however.

"So this is what happens when you get out of my sight!"

"Children cannot be spick and span and enjoy themselves as well," said Mr. Cooper.

"If I could have pigtails like Nancy and a cotton frock, I wouldn't get untidy!" complained Eva.

"Go upstairs at once!" commanded her grandmother. "You shall have a bath and go straight to bed."

"But she hasn't had any supper," Trudy reminded her.

"That is no business of yours."

Eva began to cry. "I'm hungry. I want my supper!"

"Do what you are told." The small girl went upstairs slowly, leaving consternation behind.

During supper, Trudy noticed that the salad seemed to disappear very quickly from Ping's plate. Then, at dessert, she saw him furtively secrete a stewed plum in a tin which he was hiding below the table. He caught her look.

"It's for Eva. I don't want her to starve."

"What all have you got in that tin, Ping?"

"Just a potato and a bit tomato and a piece of pudding."

"What a horrible mix up!"

"Well, it's got to be mixed up anyway, inside her. I'm going to take it up to her bedroom the minute I get the chance."

"Oh, Ping, I don't think you should!"

Nancy spoke up. "Let him do it, Trudy. It's decent of him to give up his supper."

"Yes, True, give the kid a break," pleaded David. "It's the sort of thing you'd have done yourself."

Though feeling uneasy, Trudy gave in. "But remember, Ping, it's on your own head!"

She had quite forgotten about the incident when, later on, she took Nancy and Miss Winton in to see Mrs. Stewart. The latter slipped a parcel into the invalid's hand.

"I got this for you in Dunglas Bay." It was a small bottle of lavender water. Mrs. Stewart sniffed the perfume appreciatively.

"How fresh and sweet! Like a breath of summer air. Thank you, my dear, that was a kind thought."

After sprinkling a few drops on her pillow, Olivia put the bottle on the dressing-table.

"The house has been very quiet to-day," went on Mrs. Stewart. "I missed hearing your voices. What did you do all afternoon?"

Trudy told her about their fun in the water and described the game of cricket and how Olivia had saved the side.

"I wish I was good at sport," she sighed. "All the heroines in the girls' books seem to carry their teams to victory, but I'll never do that."

"But there are different kinds of heroines."

"Look at Florence Nightingale," declared Nancy. "I'd love to be like her!"

"Many girls are heroines without knowing it," said Mrs. Stewart. "Girls who do their jobs without grumbling, girls who consider other folks' happiness before their own and who keep smiling when things go wrong."

"Perhaps that's the most difficult kind of heroine to be," observed Nancy.

Mrs. Stewart smiled at her. "Won't you give us a tune on the organ, my dear?"

Nancy complied by going over to the instrument and playing Handel's *Largo*, while the others listened intently as the slow, sweet chords swelled out to a grand melodious climax, and then faded away into silence. The resultant stillness was broken by a tap at the door, which opened a crack, and Mr. Cooper was heard to say:

"I'm sorry for intruding, but I heard music and wondered who was playing."

Mrs. Stewart bade him come in.

"How are you, Mr. Cooper?" They had met when he was on holiday last year. "I've been wondering when you were coming in to see me."

He shook hands: "Are you sure you're fit for so many visitors?"

"Certainly. I like to see people in the summer, for the winter is very quiet. Go on playing, Nancy, will you?"

The only thing that came into Nancy's head was the hymn Eva and Ping had been singing in the bus, so she played it now. "If I come to Jesus." Mrs. Stewart began to sing in a light, sweet voice, Trudy and Nancy and even Mr. Cooper joining in. Miss Winton was the only one who was silent. She sat looking out of the window, and Trudy wondered what her thoughts were.

The organ was pealing forth in fine style, when the door suddenly opened, and there on the threshold was Eva, in her nightdress and dressing-gown.

"It's my hymn! I heard it from my bed! Please, Nancy, play it again!"

To please her, Nancy repeated the melody, and the little girl began to sing by herself, shyly:

> If I come to Jesus, happy shall I be,
> He is gently calling little ones like me.

Then, with an impulsive gesture, she ran over to Trudy, raising her charming little face to hers.

"Trudy, you said you would tell me how to come to Jesus!"

Trudy put her arms round her. "Yes, dear, I'll take you upstairs. You'll get cold here, and your grandma will be annoyed."

As they left the room, hand in hand, Eva said:

"I couldn't sleep, Trudy. I felt so unhappy and I thought that if I came to Jesus, He would make me feel better." Her simplicity touched Trudy's heart.

"Yes, Eva, He makes everybody happy who believes in Him. He wants little children to come to Him, and all you have to do is to pray to Him and He will receive you."

She stopped speaking as there, on the landing, they caught sight of Eva's grandmother. She approached them angrily.

"You naughty child! What are you doing out of bed?"

Trudy made an explanation which, however, did not placate her.

"I'll not have my grand-daughter singing any of your stupid hymns! Come along, Eva, into your bed at once."

But Eva hung back. "Let Trudy come with me, please! She's going to tell me about Jesus."

Mrs. Somers glared at Trudy.

"I did ask you to stop talking about your religion, didn't I? There's been nothing but trouble since Eva met you. To-night I found that your precious little brother had actually defied me by bringing her food in bed!"

"I'm sorry. Ping only did it out of kindness."

"We don't want kindness from any of you. Please leave Eva and go downstairs. Good-night!"

Eva stood forlornly, her eyes full of tears. Trudy stooped to kiss her: "Good-night, darling. Don't be unhappy. Jesus will be with you."

"Good-night," repeated Mrs. Somers, whisking Eva away.

Trudy went slowly to her room, troubled in mind. Following a custom which her mother had taught her, she got down on her knees and asked God to comfort little Eva and to bring Mrs. Somers to a better understanding of her charge. Prayer always eased her mind of its burden. Though she could see no way out of the dilemma, she knew that God would have a way of His own.

CHAPTER X

Adventure for Ping

MRS. STEWART was to have still another visitor that evening. As Trudy came downstairs from her bedroom, she heard a ring at the bell, and to save Miss Stewart trouble, she opened the door herself. There, smiling all over his bronzed, handsome face, was Brian Clyde.

"It's my friend Trudy. How is Mrs. Stewart to-night?"

"Very well. She'll be delighted to see you."

He entered the room like a cool, refreshing breeze.

"Brian!" cried the invalid. "Well, well, I'm holding court to-night, sure enough. Do you know Miss Winton? Yes, of course you do. You rescued her on the stepping-stones."

Olivia's face flushed a delightful pink, as she laid her hand in his.

"Feeling any the worse?" he asked.

"Not at all. Very much better."

Mr. Cooper also shook hands. "If you don't mind, I'll go and join my wife now," he told Mrs. Stewart.

"Bring her in to see me sometime, will you?"

"I'll ask her. But she keeps to herself a lot since—"

"I know. But that may not be good for her. I'd like a talk with her."

After Mr. Cooper left, Nancy said good-night,

too, and the four remaining settled down for a long
talk, which at length veered round to David's
picture on the wall.

"I was attracted by it whenever I came in," said
Brian Clyde, studying it with an experienced eye.
"It has some youthful faults, but shows great promise.
How old is your brother, Trudy?"

"Seventeen," she told him.

"I'm interested in young fellows who take their
painting seriously. I'd like to have a talk with
David, perhaps give him a few hints. Is he in
the house?"

"No, he'll be in the tent, I think. Shall I fetch
him?"

But he said he was going home that way and
would probably see him. Then he went over and
took Mrs. Stewart's hand in his, looking deep into
her serene blue eyes:

"Whenever I feel tired and a little hopeless,
I think of you lying here. In the town where I live
in the winter, everything is rush and bustle. People
are so busy, they have no time to think where it is all
leading them, and I picture you in this little room,
with your Bible below your pillow and your mind
dwelling on the lovely things it contains. I want
to say to these bustling people: 'Be quiet a little
while and let the world go on without you.'"

"Why don't you say it, Brian?"

"I do, but my words are lost in the din." He
sighed. "More and more I feel as if I want to
devote my life to telling the poor harassed folk of
to-day that they are going the wrong way about
solving their problems. My text would be simple
the words of Jesus—'I am the Way, the Truth,
and the Life.'"

Trudy and Miss Winton sat very still. Mrs. Stewart laid her hand on top of Brian's: "If you feel that is your mission, Brian, I hope you will carry it out some day. My blessing will go with you."

When he took his leave, Trudy accompanied him across the field, saying very little, for she could see that he was engrossed in his thoughts. They found David at the tent, busy securing some pegs that had come loose. As he straightened himself, he noted with surprise the tall figure of Trudy's companion.

"This is David, Mr. Clyde."

"I am glad to meet a fellow artist." Brian held out his hand.

"I can't call myself an artist yet," said David.

"Oh, yes, you can. That picture of Rocky Point merits praise."

David's face lit up. "You saw my picture?"

"I did. Perhaps you would like to come round to my studio to-morrow afternoon, and we could have a talk about art."

"I'd like nothing better!"

Having said good-night, Brian Clyde strode away in the direction of Waterside. David watched him admiringly.

"There goes a real man!"

"I've never known anyone like him," agreed Trudy. "And to think, if you had sold your picture to Mr. Cooper, he might never have seen it."

The realization made David very thoughtful. He was thankful he had not sold his picture. The friendship of Brian Clyde was worth more to him than any amount of money.

He went to sleep very happy that night, and even Ping's restlessness did not disturb him.

Next morning, Ping awoke very early. He hated lying still when he could not sleep, so he slid out of the blankets and put on his clothes. Rusty was awake too, sitting alert, his tail thumping on the ground. David turned sleepily: "Is it time to get up?"

"Not for ages," Ping assured him, so he relapsed into slumber.

Then Ping crept out of the tent, followed by Rusty. Outside, everything was very still. A low, summery mist lay over the water and the dew was fresh on the grass. The sea was so calm that the rocks were reflected in it as in a mirror. Ping drew in deep breaths of the fresh, morning air. Standing there on the slope of the field with not another person in sight, he felt as if the world was his.

With a glad whoop, he leapt across the grass towards the beach. Lifting a piece of stick, he threw it with all his might into the water. It fell with a light splash and floated on the surface like a fairy boat.

"Fetch it, Rusty!" he called.

The puppy raced to the sea's edge and into the water. He did not like it much at first, but Ping urged him on. "Fetch it, boy!"

The short legs thrashed at the water until Rusty suddenly discovered that he was able to swim. Straight as a die he paddled towards the stick, caught it in his mouth, and brought it back to Ping's feet. The experiment was repeated until both dog and boy got tired of the sport. Then Ping looked round for further inspiration. In the dis-

tance, he saw Rocky Point stretching far out into
the water, etched against the sky just as it was in
David's picture.

Then he remembered about the cave, and the man
who slept on a bed of bracken. Was his 'convict'
still around? Now was the time to catch him, in
the early morning before he had a chance to disappear. He would have to go round by the shore,
of course, the way he and Trudy had gone the other
night; but the prospect did not deter him. Calling
on Rusty, he set off, feeling like a detective accompanied by his bloodhound.

The going was hard, but, braced by the sense of
adventure, he scarcely felt it. Half a dozen times
he tripped and fell, acquiring new cuts and bruises
at every turn. When at length he drew near the
cave, he went warily. If the convict heard him
coming, the game was lost.

Now he was creeping through the narrow alley
at the mouth of the cave.

"Ssh, Rusty!" he whispered, and the dog slunk
along as quietly as his master. Now, he thought,
to peep in and see if the convict was there. Was
that the sound of breathing? He had often heard
the same kind of breathing when he stood outside
Dad's bedroom at home. He stepped forward
and peeped into the cave, his heart leaping and
thudding when he saw that the bracken bed was
still there, and on it the figure of a man fast asleep!

Now that he had really found his convict, Ping
did not feel quite so adventurous. Indeed, he
was ready to take to his heels and run, when Rusty
let out a sharp bark and the man stirred in his sleep
and sat up with a jerk.

"Who's that? Who is there?"

In a very small voice, Ping replied: "It's only me."

The man stared at him and Ping stared back at his bushy red beard. "Well, if it isn't the young shaver that wanted to travel the world! Where did you spring from at this time of day?"

"I woke up early and came round to see you, please," faltered Ping.

"But how did you know I was here?"

"I saw your bed one day and thought you were an escaped convict."

"And what if I am?" asked the man.

"I'll help you," promised Ping, eagerly. "I can bring you food from the farm."

"That's swell of you." He rose and stretched himself to his full height. Ping studied him thoughtfully.

"Don't you take off your clothes at night? I wish I could go to bed with my clothes on, but they won't let me."

"Wait till you're a man and you'll be able to do what you like, perhaps! So you live at Stewart's farm. How is Mrs. Stewart, can you tell me?"

Ping's face sobered. "She's got to lie in her bed all day. She had an accident."

"Yes. I heard about that. And Mr. Stewart?"

"He's not so nice as Mrs. Stewart, but Trudy says he's all right, deep down."

"H'm." The man was at the fireplace now, raking it out and building a fire with dry kindling, to which he set a match. "Like to have breakfast with me, boy?"

"Oh, yes, yes!"

"Then you'll find a spring up on the hill there. Here's a kettle and a cup to fill it with." From a hidden niche high up in the cave wall he took the utensils. Ping raced up to the spring, full of self importance. This was adventure at last! When he came back the cave-man had emptied a tin of beans into a billycan and set it on the fire.

That was a wonderful breakfast—baked beans and oatcakes, washed down by a strong brew of tea and flavoured by tales of foreign countries that made Ping's eyes grow big.

"I'd love to be an explorer and go where there are no roads and no houses!"

"Well, you could do that here. You were exploring when you came along the beach, weren't you? You need a good sense of direction when you're on the hills, though. It's best to carry a compass."

"What's a compass?" asked Ping.

"A thing with a pointer, like a watch. It always points to the north, and by that you know the other directions."

"I see. I'd like to have a compass." They chatted on, till Ping suddenly blurted out:

"Have you really been in prison?"

His friend gave a twisted smile. "I'm sorry to disillusion you, Ping, but that is one place where I've never been, though I've often felt desperate enough."

"Then, if you're not an escaped convict, why are you hiding here?"

"I just came here for—call it a holiday. I was going to leave the island yesterday, but something made me change my mind. However, that's another story, and I think I've told you plenty. Won't your family be looking for you? It's after eight o'clock."

Ping got up reluctantly, calling for Rusty, who had disappeared on a rabbit hunt. "Trudy will be getting all flapped up. She makes such a fuss, you'd think she was my mother!"

"It was Trudy who gave me the rose yesterday, wasn't it?"

Ping hated to tear himself away. "May I come back to-morrow?"

"I'm afraid not. I'd rather folk didn't know I was here. You can keep a secret, can't you?"

"Sure, I can."

"They'd soon find out about me if you made a habit of coming here before breakfast. No, Ping, you'd better forget about me."

Ping's face fell. "I'll try," he said mournfully, as he turned away. The cave-man called him back.

"I've just thought of something. Next time you come here, through the day, just have a look on the ledge inside the cave. I'll leave something for you."

Ping brightened. "Truly? That'll be tops!"

As he picked his way along the shore, he turned every now and again to wave to his friend. He hoped he would see him again, sometime, but it might just lead to discovery, and Ping wasn't going to be the one to give him away.

When he reached the tent at last, it was quite empty, and he could hear the breakfast gong ringing. He broke into a run.

Trudy and David were waiting at the door, wondering what had become of him. He explained that he had been 'round the shore,' and was chased up to the bathroom to make himself presentable.

When he came down to breakfast, he found, to his surprise, that he was not hungry. Halfway through his porridge he declared that he could not eat another bite. Trudy was worried.

"But after all that fresh air, you ought to be hungry, Ping!"

"I don't like porridge very well," he replied. "I think we should have something else for breakfast. Baked beans; the kind that come out of a tin."

"Whatever gave you that idea?"

Ping hugged his secret. "Just. I like baked beans."

Trudy concluded that the ice-cream yesterday had upset him.

"If you're not hungry by lunch time, we'll have to give you some medicine."

Ping was alarmed, but fortunately, by lunchtime his appetite had reached normal proportions, and Trudy's anxiety was allayed.

There was another letter from home that day. Trudy read it to the others, except for one passage which she thought it best to keep to herself meantime. She took Nancy into her confidence, however.

"Bad news, Nancy. Ping's puss has been run over by a car. Mum got to hear about it in a roundabout way, but there's no doubt it was Abednego. I don't know how to break it to him."

"Let him enjoy his holiday," advised Nancy. "We can tell him on the last day."

It seemed the best way, though Trudy knew it would be on her mind for the rest of their stay at Ardensheel. However, Ping was so happy at the moment, she could not bear to think of his holiday being spoiled, so she and Nancy decided to keep the knowledge to themselves.

CHAPTER XI

A Wet Afternoon

IT was too showery that afternoon to go to Silver Beach, so Nancy and Trudy were taking advantage of a bright spell to sit outside on the lawn. David had gone off in high spirits to visit Brian Clyde, and Ping and Eva were looking at picture books in the lounge.

"There's Mr. Cooper," whispered Nancy as the house door opened and he came out, dressed in his raincoat, and looking hurriedly at his watch. Seeing them he said:

"I'd like a word with you, girls. I've been called back to town for a few days, and I'm afraid my wife will be lonely. I thought perhaps I might leave her in Miss Winton's charge, but I can't find her. Will you be a friend to her, Trudy?"

He looked so worried, Trudy replied instantly. "Of course, Mr. Cooper."

"And you, Nancy? I know it's a lot to ask of young girls, but you two are more thoughtful and considerate than most. Thank you so much." After shaking hands, he strode off to catch the bus, with an anxious look on his face.

Trudy felt as if he had laid a responsibility on her. It was going to be difficult to befriend Mrs. Cooper. All her advances hitherto had been repulsed, and yet, she must make another effort.

She went straight to Mrs. Stewart's room, to see if Miss Winton might be there, but the invalid was alone.

"Have you seen Miss Winton, Mrs. Stewart?"

"Not to-day. Are you worried about something, dear?"

"Not worried exactly." She told her about Mr. Cooper's request. "How can I befriend Mrs. Cooper? She puts up a barrier every time I speak to her."

"I wish she would come in to see me. I feel so sorry for her. Could you ask her, Trudy?"

Trudy thought there would be no harm trying, so she went in search of Mrs. Cooper. She found her in a corner of the lounge reading a book and apparently taking no interest whatever in the amusing chatter of Ping and Eva. Mrs. Somers was also there, guarding her grand-daughter as usual from possible harm. Since last night, Trudy had not had a chance to speak to Eva alone.

Plucking up courage, she said to Mrs. Cooper in a low voice: "Mrs. Stewart says you haven't been in to see her yet. Could you pay her a little visit just now? She's very lonely, and loves someone to talk to."

Mrs. Cooper was taken aback.

"I'm not a very good conversationalist, I'm afraid."

"That doesn't matter. She's easy to talk to. Please!" She put all her heart into the request. Mrs. Cooper rose reluctantly. "Very well, for a few minutes."

Trudy accompanied her into the room. Mrs. Stewart's face glowed a welcome as she held out a hand.

"I'm so happy to see you, my dear. You've been hiding yourself away since you came."

The other flushed. "I haven't felt like company, Mrs. Stewart."

Feeling that they were best left alone, Trudy slipped out of the room.

Mrs. Stewart studied the face of her visitor who was sitting with an absent look in her eyes, as if her thoughts were far away. This was a mere shell of a woman, a creature who walked and talked mechanically, as if something vital within her had been destroyed.

"I, too, have been through the valley of the shadow," whispered the invalid. "Don't stay in the darkness too long, my dear. Let in the light. It is there, if you will only see it."

"There is no light," was the low response.

"Once I said the same, but the light came. It is in the Book—" she laid her hand on her Bible. "'Christ shall give thee light.' Forgive me for asking, but are you a Believer, my dear?"

"I was," she said, "up till the time I lost my little girl. But how am I to believe any more?"

"Hold on to your faith, and the path will be made plain. No-one gets through life without trial and sorrow. Some folk sink under it; others can overcome. Christ helps us to overcome. Have you given Him a chance?"

The weeping woman shook her head dumbly.

"Ask Him to help you. Keep on asking. He will not fail you."

"If I thought it would do any good," murmured the other.

"It will. I am sure of that. And you have not only yourself to think of, you know; there is your husband. He must have felt the blow as much as you. Have you tried to comfort him?"

The question was unexpected. She looked up in surprise.

"I never thought of it. It has always been he who has tried to comfort me."

"He is a good man," said the other, "and he must be suffering greatly."

"But he talks and even laughs, the same as he used to. Sometimes I think he doesn't care."

"That is because he is brave as well as good. It can't be easy for him to put a cheerful face on grief. A man like him deserves an equally fine helpmate, my dear."

"Oh!" cried Mrs. Cooper, getting to her feet. "Please don't torment me like this! As if I didn't know I'm not good enough for him!"

"You can be, with God's help," was the soft reply. "You have been keeping your bitterness stored up too long. Let it out, on your knees. Tell God everything."

The sorrowful woman stood drooping by the bedside.

"There's something hard around my heart that prevents me; but I'll try, Mrs. Stewart, I'll try. Good-bye, and thank you."

With an impulsive gesture, Agnes Cooper bent down and kissed the smooth brow of the invalid. Then she went swiftly upstairs to her own room. There she immediately knelt down by the bedside, releasing her pent-up feelings in a cry for help from the God she had once believed in. Gradually, her emotions were calmed and she felt strength flow into her, strength from that highest Source which she had not appealed to in vain. When she got to her feet, she was mistress of herself again, humbly penitent for her failure towards the man whom she truly loved, and determined to make the future atone for the past.

Meanwhile, Trudy had put on her raincoat and waterproof head square, and gone out alone for a walk in the rain which was now falling in a steady downpour.

As she trudged along the country road she reflected on the difference between a wet day in the country and in the town, where everything was so grey and miserable. Here, the mist on the hills had a picturesque quality that soaking roofs could never have; the sea came rolling over the empty beach in long waves edged with white foam, and grass and hedges seemed to be saying 'thank you' for the moisture which meant new life to them.

Wet drips trickled down her neck, and her shoes began to squelch, but what did she care? She had other shoes, and her things would soon dry in the laundry off the kitchen. Lifting her eyes she observed someone coming towards her; another crazy person who liked to walk in the rain! She was quite close before she recognized Olivia Winton.

In spite of her dripping condition, Olivia greeted her brightly. "Don't you love this, Trudy, walking in the rain?"

"Yes, I do." Trudy took her friend's arm and turned back with her. "I wondered where you had disappeared to, Miss Winton."

"Couldn't you call me Olivia? Miss Winton sounds so stiff."

"I'd love to. Olivia is such a pretty name, much nicer than Gertrude, which is what they called me."

"I like 'Gertrude,' though Trudy sounds friendlier. I've been out since lunch time, Trudy. I wanted to get away alone to think. Did you ever feel like that?"

Trudy admitted that it was a habit of hers, too.

"Some people don't like being alone with themselves. I wonder why it is?"

"I think it's because they are afraid of their thoughts. I have been afraid of my own thoughts, up till recently."

"And you're not afraid now?"

"No. I'll tell you something, Trudy. Something happened to me to-day, just a little while ago. I was walking in the direction of the stepping-stones and thinking about the things Mrs. Stewart had talked about, and of yourself and Brian Clyde —three happy people whose lives are an example to other folk. There must be something in this religion of yours, I thought; something that might give me strength to face the future." There was a calm, uplifted look on her face. They walked on for some moments before she went on:

"When I came to the stepping-stones, I stood for a long time, remembering my feelings the other day. One moment, I was standing terror-stricken, with the water swirling round me; the next, I felt safe and unafraid, because Brian Clyde was there and I could lean on him. Then," she continued, "I suddenly realized that Jesus was like that; that the terror of my soul could be stilled if only I would trust Him."

Trudy pressed her arm.

"I'm so glad, Olivia, that you have come to feel that. I know it's the only way to be happy. If you could meet my mother, she would explain better than I can."

"Someday I'll come and see your mother, Trudy. I still feel a little bit lost and unsure, and wondered if you could lend me your Bible for a day or two.

I think it would help me. It's so long since I
opened one, and after hearing that Psalm the other
night, I'm sure I'll find an answer to a great many
things there."

"I'm sure you will, Olivia," Trudy promised
willingly.

They had reached the house now, and Trudy had
just time to change into dry clothes before the tea-
bell rang. David had not yet come back from
Waterside, so they guessed that he would be having
tea with Brian Clyde.

Ping munched hungrily at the home-made scones
with fresh butter. In spite of his two breakfasts
and large lunch, his appetite was as hearty as ever.

"Do you like the scones?" asked Nancy.

"Best I ever tasted. Miss Stewart's a wizard
cook."

"Allow me to inform you—" Nancy's chin went
up—"that these scones were baked by ME."

Ping would not believe it. "But the scones you
make at home are like bits of leather!"

"This was Miss Stewart's secret recipe. It's
been handed down from her great-grandmother."

"They really are good," agreed Trudy. "Congratulations, kid. I can see you're going to beat
me hollow."

"Oh, well, you can always write poetry," was the
condescending reply.

"Poetry won't feed you when you're hungry,"
Ping had to observe. "I expect you're a 'Mary,'
Trudy, and Nancy's a 'Martha.'"

It was a good summing up of the two girls'
characters, though Trudy undoubtedly had some
'Martha' qualities as well. Thinking and dreaming
would, however, always come first with her.

"Mr. Stewart says we'll have to sleep in the shed to-night," Ping said again. "The tent's all soppy. Even if you only touch the roof with your wee finger, it leaks."

"Then don't touch it," Nancy told him. "I don't envy you, sleeping in the shed. There's sure to be rats there. They'll bite your toes."

"I'm not afraid of rats like girls are," declared her brother.

Some time later David came back. His eyes were shining and he looked on top of the world. He tried to give Trudy an idea of what the afternoon had meant to him.

"Brian Clyde's studio is an artist's dream, Trudy! He showed me some of his recent paintings. They're so wonderful, they made me feel just a dauber; but he says I show promise. He's interested in me!"

"That's grand, David."

"I've to go and see him every day, if I like. If he is busy painting, I can mooch around on my own, he says. He's going to show me how to use oils and let me into the secrets of scraper-board—that black and white stuff, you know. The time's simply going to race!"

Trudy was very glad for him. She had been a bit worried in case David would feel lonely, but now there was no chance of that.

"It's not only because he's an artist that I admire him," he went on. "Do you know what he has been telling me, True? He's almost decided to confine his painting to the summer months, and for the rest of the year he's going to carry on a mission in the busy towns, just travelling round preaching, where he thinks it will do most good."

"Yes, I heard him telling Mrs. Stewart. There aren't enough of his kind in the world, David."

Writing home that night, she said:

"To-morrow is Sunday. We have been here for nearly a week. It seems longer than that, somehow. The others are writing to you, too. Nancy will tell you about the scones she baked. They were wizard. David has made friends with Brian Clyde; he is more enthusiastic than I've ever known him. Ping has been very excited all day, the way he acts at home when he has some secret or other. I suppose we'll find out what it is some-time. I haven't told him the bad news about Abednego yet; poor Ping, he will miss his cat very much.

"Miss Winton says I have to call her 'Olivia.' She is beginning to feel happier, Mum, and the faith she used to have as a child has come back to her. I'm so glad about it, as I like her so much. But I'm not so happy about Eva. Her grand-mother won't allow me to speak to the child alone, in case I fill her head with 'religion.' It's very difficult, Mum. I wonder what you would do in my place?

"I must tell you about the man with the red beard that we met in Dunglas Bay yesterday—"

Her pen ran on, trying to keep up with her thoughts. She knew her mother would be inter-ested, for she had the gift of sympathy with young and old. Although she was enjoying her holiday, Trudy was already longing to see her parents again, and she knew that when their last day came, she would not be altogether sorry to go home.

CHAPTER XII

More Trouble for Eva

NEXT day was Sunday. In the forenoon the four Lawsons went to the picturesque old church in the village. The afternoon was spent quietly on the lawn where Brian Clyde joined them. He and Olivia Winton talked about their experiences in the Middle East, while the others listened with interest.

After tea, Brian held a short service in Mrs. Stewart's room. Trudy was happy to see Mrs. Cooper present. What Mrs. Stewart had said to her, Trudy did not know, but she seemed to be a changed woman. Though still very quiet, she was certainly making an effort to be more sociable, and once or twice a smile lit up her face, giving it a softness and beauty that had not been there before. Only one thing could account for this change. She must have gone for comfort and strength to the God who had helped Mrs. Stewart in her own trouble and who, Trudy knew, would help her too when the need arose.

At breakfast next morning, Ping begged David to take them for a row in the *Stella Maris*. It was such a lovely morning and the water looked so inviting, that he could not refuse. Olivia said she would join them, and the five of them made their way down to the cove where the boat lay. They had all taken their places except David, when a small figure appeared from behind a rock.

"I want to come too," said Eva.

The sad little face looked very appealing.

"Have you asked your grandmother?" enquired Trudy.

Eva's toe poked about in the gravel. "She said I could come if I wanted to."

"Let her come," pleaded Ping. "She gets no fun at all."

The others said the same. Trudy could not bear to send the child away, so she was allowed to sit in the bow along with Ping. When they reached Rocky Point, Ping was extremely anxious to go ashore, so they disembarked in the inlet near the cave.

While Nancy and Trudy bathed and David lay on a flat rock planning his next picture, Olivia Winton sat alone on the turf that fringed the beach. Opening Trudy's Bible which she had brought with her, she read the words:

'God is our refuge and strength, a very present help in trouble; therefore will not we fear though the earth be removed and though the mountains be carried into the midst of the sea.'

She read on, refreshing her thirsty soul, gathering conviction with every word as the real meaning of God's goodness grew within her. God had sent His only begotten Son to save people like her who, deceived by the things of the world, had been left stranded and hopeless. The wonder of it made her heart swell within her.

While she sat there, oblivious to all that was going on around her, Ping had also gone away on his own. He was so eager to get to the cave that he almost tripped over himself in his hurry. There was no sign of the cave-man anywhere, though a heap of bracken still lay at the cave mouth. But he had promised to leave him a message, hadn't he? The red-bearded hero was not the kind of person to forget a promise.

Eva followed him, curious. It was the first time she had been here, and her eyes were like shining lights.

"Is this your cave, Ping?"

"Yes, but go away. You can't come here."

"Why not?"

"It's a secret. Run and watch Trudy bathing. I'll let you see into the cave afterwards."

She left him reluctantly.

In an instant Ping was heaping stone upon stone, so that he could stand up to reach the hidden ledge where the cave-man kept his things. Ah, there it was; a parcel tied up with string with a label attached: "FOR PING."

Excitedly he opened it. Inside a small box was a thing like a watch with a pointer which wobbled when you moved it. There was a note, too.

"Dear Ping,—This is a compass. It always points to what is called the 'magnetic north.' Use it to get your bearings. It is a great thing, Ping, to know where you are going in life and to be able to travel straight.—Your Cave Man."

Ping was entranced with the gift. He would have loved to rush out and show it to the others, but that meant giving away his secret. So he put it into his pocket for the time being, but during the day, whenever he was alone, he took it out to consult it.

Feeling rather hurt by being ordered off, Eva wandered along the shore. By this time, Trudy had had enough of the water and had put on her clothes again. She was shaking out her damp hair when Eva came along. It was the first time she had had a chance to get the child to herself.

"What, all alone?"

She nodded. "Ping's got a secret he doesn't want me to share."

"Poor kid." Trudy sat down on a stone and took Eva beside her. "You often feel lonely, don't you?"

"Yes, Trudy. I wish my Dad and Mum would come home from India."

"Never mind. When you are a big, strong girl you can go out and live with them."

"I get so frightened at night in my bed alone. Trudy, you said Jesus would be with me. What did you mean by that? I can't see Him anywhere."

"No, darling. You see, Jesus lived in the world a long time ago and He was put to death by wicked men. But, being the Son of God death had no hold over Him, and He rose from the dead. If we believe in Him, we shall likewise be victors over death."

Eva's eyes were full of wonder. "Tell me more, Trudy."

"Jesus still lives to-day. Though we can't see Him, we can feel His presence in our hearts. If you open your heart and let Him in, He will make you very, very happy."

"Is that what you call 'coming to Jesus'?"

"Yes, dear. When you go to bed to-night, kneel down and pray. Tell Jesus you want Him to come into your heart and into your life and make you good like Himself. Will you do that, Eva?"

"Yes, Trudy, I will."

"And here is something for you to say." Trudy repeated slowly the lines:

Gentle Jesus, meek and mild,
Look upon a little child;
Pity my simplicity,
Suffer me to come to Thee.

Eva said the words after her, till she had them
by heart.

"I'll say it every time I feel lonely, Trudy.   It
will just be like speaking to a Friend."   She threw
her arms round Trudy's neck and kissed her.   "I
like you.   You are kind and good.   I wish you
were my sister."

As the smooth cheek was laid against hers,
Trudy felt full of love and pity, not only for Eva,
but for all the children like her who had no-one to
lead them in the right way.

Soon it was time to leave and, the wind being in
their favour, David swiftly rowed them home.   As
he manoeuvred the boat into the shallow waters of
the cove, they saw Mrs. Somers standing waiting
on the beach.   Her face was grim with annoyance.
Eva grew pale and trembled.

"I told a lie," she said.   "Grandma said I was
not to go with you."

It was just what Trudy had feared.

"You shouldn't tell lies, Eva.   But we'll stick
by you, don't worry."

Mrs. Somers came forward to meet them, her
eyes blazing:

"How dare you go with these people when I
expressly forbade you?" she exclaimed.   "You
shall come upstairs with me and go to bed for the
rest of the day!"

Pale, but determined, Trudy intervened.

"No, Mrs. Somers, please!   That's not the way

to treat Eva.   You restrict her too much; no wonder she disobeys!"

"Nobody asked for your opinion.   I suppose you encouraged her to go, so that you could cram your religion down her throat!"

"No, I didn't do that."   She managed to keep her voice calm.   "I just told her some things that might comfort her when she is unhappy.   But I'm quite willing to take all the blame of her coming with us.   It was really my fault.   It wouldn't be fair to punish Eva."

"Trudy is right," declared Olivia.   "It is we who are to blame."

David spoke up impetuously as he did when roused.   "You're a cruel old woman!   If you put Eva to bed, we'll come upstairs too and keep her company!"

"Yes," added Ping, "and we'll bring her up lots of food to keep her from starving!"

Mrs. Somers could only gasp.   Then, with a speechless glance she caught Eva's hand and walked her up to the house.

"If Eva doesn't come down for lunch, we'll all go upstairs in a body.   Are you all game?" announced David.

Rather doubtfully, they promised.   The atmosphere was tense as they sat in the dining-room, waiting.   Trudy's thoughts were in a turmoil.   She was on Eva's side, but a stand-up battle was the last thing she wanted.   There surely was some other way to bring Mrs. Somers round to a better frame of mind?

It did not come to a stand-up fight, however. Probably Mrs. Somers did not want such a thing any more than they did.   She had seen that their threats were not idle ones, and for once she gave way, bringing Eva down to lunch, so that the Lawsons gave each other a glance of triumph and relief. The trouble was not over, however. Trudy felt that the heated argument had made the old lady more unfriendly than ever. It looked as if her enmity might shadow the remainder of their holiday.

Eva was not allowed to accompany them to the Silver Beach in the afternoon, which was only to be expected. Mrs. Cooper, however, volunteered to come with them, and proved herself quite a charming companion, though there were times when she would fall into a sad silence that made Trudy very sorry for her. She wondered what would happen when Mr. Cooper came back. Would his wife treat him coldly as before, or would her softened mood include him as well?

She had not long to wait to find out. When they returned from the beach, they found that Mr. Cooper had got back sooner than he had expected. He was sitting on the garden seat with Eva, showing her how to make rush baskets. When she saw him, his wife's face paled over and she grasped Trudy's arm as if for support. Mr. Cooper rose and came forward.

"Hello, everybody!"

Trudy's eyes were on Mrs. Cooper's face, which had now flushed scarlet. But she returned her husband's greeting and laid her hand in his, smiling at him with love in her eyes.

"I'm so glad you're back, Robert."

Trudy saw his face light up with a wonderful happiness as he drew her arm through his and walked with her into the house. Truly, that hour in Mrs. Stewart's room had worked a miracle in the lives of these two. The barriers between them had melted away, and though the sadness of loss was still in their hearts, it was a burden they could bear together, fortified by a higher faith.

That evening, as usual, Trudy visited the boys' tent to hear Ping say his prayers. To-night he made a special point of asking God's blessing for his 'cave man.'

"I don't believe there's any cave man," laughed Trudy as she tucked him in. "He's just a creature of your imagination."

"No, Trudy, he's real. I know, because—" he stopped short.

"He's real in your imagination, you mean?" She bent over to kiss him good-night. "Go to sleep now, and be fresh for more adventures to-morrow." His pillow was crushed, so she took it up to straighten it. Ping made a clutch at it, but it was too late to hide the secret that was disclosed below.

"What's this?" Trudy picked up the cave man's present and looked at it curiously. Ping grabbed it out of her hand.

"It's a compass. That's what it is."

"But where did you get it, Ping?"

"I—I found it," he stammered. "I found it in the cave."

"Oh, Ping, are you sure? But even if you did, it's not yours, you know."

"It is mine, Trudy; really, it is."

She felt that he was hiding something from her.

"Won't you tell me the truth about it, Ping?"

"I have told you the truth," he gulped, and not another word of explanation could she get out of him.

Leaving him for the night, she walked back to the house feeling quite disturbed. She hoped that Ping had not done anything wrong. The compass was just the sort of thing a boy would get his eye on and crave for his own. What if Ping had actually stolen it from somewhere? But the boy knew right from wrong so well; and he had never done anything like that before.

All the same, she could not help but worry. Life was a queer mix-up of rough and smooth, she reflected. Even on holiday things never went right for long at a time. No sooner had something good turned up, than something bad came along to counteract it. She had been so happy to think that life had become brighter for Olivia and Mrs. Cooper; but to-day she seemed to have made an enemy of Mrs. Somers, and now, here was this mystery about Ping.

CHAPTER XIII

Adventure with a Shark

NEXT forenoon, Trudy and Olivia went round to Waterside by the stepping-stones and listened to the service, after which Brian Clyde showed them round his studio and introduced them to a few of his summer guests. Trudy observed that the eyes of these friends followed him about everywhere, as if they loved him and were longing to serve him.

"He gives out a kind of radiance; or perhaps you might call it magnetism. Do you feel it, Olivia?"

Her companion nodded.

"It's partly his personality, and partly his convictions. The one is made more shining by the other. When he speaks I want to do nothing but listen, on and on."

Trudy understood what she meant.

"I'd like to come back here every day," said Olivia on the way home. "Do you think he would mind?"

"I'm sure he wouldn't."

"I'll never forget how he said to me, that first day—'You will be better soon.' I think he meant I'd be better in soul as well as in body."

As Ping had never been to Waterside, except in the boat, David promised to take him there in the afternoon. Nancy had a date in the kitchen, where Miss Stewart was going to teach her to make savoury pancakes.

The rest of the guests were sitting on the lawn after lunch, when Mr. Cooper suggested that they might go for a row in the *Stella Maris*.

"How about it, Trudy?"

"Yes, I'd like to, Mr. Cooper."

"Me, too!" exclaimed Eva. Her grandmother frowned.

"Certainly not!" she remonstrated, knitting furiously.

"Why not let her come, Mrs. Somers? I'll take good care of her," Mr. Cooper assured her.

Mrs. Somers glared at Trudy. "I don't know what may happen if I let her out of my sight."

"But you don't need to. You can come too."

She looked dubiously down at the rowing-boat.

"I don't care for small boats, but if it's a short sail I may as well go with you." With a bad grace, she rolled up her knitting.

"Count me out, please," said Olivia. "I have some letters to write."

"You will come, Agnes?" to his wife.

"Of course, Robert. I'll put on my swimming suit."

He looked pleased, for it was the first time she had bathed this summer.

As they rowed out from the bay, Olivia waved to them from the lawn. No hint of disaster was in her mind, nor in the minds of any of them. It was just another sail in the boat which they had used practically every day since their arrival. Mr. Cooper was a capable oarsman, and the sea was as calm as glass. What could possibly happen to them?

Poor Eva was obliged to sit beside her grandmother, as still as a statue. Trudy herself was in the bow, Mr. Cooper at the oars, and Mrs. Cooper in the stern with the two others.

As they sailed towards Rocky Point, Eva pointed her finger out to sea:

"There's a funny thing in the water over there."

"Where?" they asked, turning to look.

"It's gone now, but I saw it. It was a black thing sticking out of the water and it was sailing along."

"What nonsense," grumbled her grandmother.

They soon forgot about the curious object, however, and had almost reached Rocky Point when suddenly, quite close to them, there was the most tremendous splash they had ever heard. For an instant they got a glimpse of a curved black body diving deep into the water, and their faces were covered with spray.

Even Mr. Cooper turned pale, though he tried to reassure the others.

"It's one of these basking sharks we've heard about. I'd better row for the shore. There's no need to panic; they're not dangerous."

He meant that the creature would not harm them knowingly; but unfortunately, the shark had been scared by the motion of the boat and had lost its sense of direction. Though Mr. Cooper immediately made for the shore, the shark must have done likewise, for after a few moments, it tried to surface underneath the boat. All they knew was that something hit the keel a dreadful blow, and then the boat rocked horribly, throwing them all to one side. Before they could recover themselves, the boat overturned, throwing them into the water.

Trudy found herself choking down salt water as she battled frantically for air. After swimming

a few strokes, she felt she could not keep it up, for,
light as they were, she was impeded by her clothes.
Strange that there should come to her at that
moment the memory of Nancy's voice, saying:

"Lie on your back and float."

Somehow, she managed to turn on her back.
Remembering Nancy's advice, she kept her head
well back and let herself relax. To her surprise
she soon found that she was actually floating; in
fact, in spite of the terrible situation, there was
something almost pleasant about it.

But what about the others? She could hear
splashes, voices, confusion. It was dreadful to
know that she could do nothing for anybody.
What would she have given at this moment to be
a strong swimmer and be able to save people's
lives!

She seemed to lie there for a very long time,
unable to keep count of what was going on around
her, and telling herself that she must not feel afraid
or she would begin to sink. Please God, make me
brave, she breathed; and the silent prayer steadied
and calmed her. After what seemed hours, she
heard someone swimming towards her, and a man's
voice sounded very near:

"Keep as you are. Don't struggle or splash.
I'm going to tow you to the shore."

"The others," gasped Trudy. "I'm all right.
Please save the others!"

"The others are being taken care of. You do as
you're told."

She felt a pair of hands beneath her head, strong
limbs cleaving the water below her. Then she was
propelled slowly shorewards. She had seen Nancy
practising this method of life-saving, little knowing

that one day she was to have direct experience!

The whole incident seemed so unreal that it had not surprised her to observe, with the one glimpse she had got of her rescuer's face, that it was the red-bearded man she had given the rose to at Dunglas Bay.

Perhaps, after all, it was a horrid dream, and she would wake up to find herself beside Nancy under the cam-ceiling at Ardensheel. But no, this was reality all right. They were in shallow water now, and her rescuer was helping her to her feet. Mrs. Cooper, dripping wet in her bathing suit, took her hands and guided her ashore. They were in the inlet beside the cave.

"Very good, Trudy. You kept your head. How do you feel?"

"I'm fine, thanks. Wh-what happened to everybody?"

Looking round she saw poor little Eva sitting on a rock crying bitterly, her clothes saturated with water. Mr. Cooper was kneeling on the ground beside the prostrate figure of Mrs. Somers.

"I think she must have got a blow on the head as the boat overturned," said Mrs. Cooper. "My husband clung to the boat and held her up while I swam with Eva to the beach."

"You did a splendid job swimming out again for the old lady," said the red-bearded man.

"Still, it's a good thing you saw us from the shore. I suppose we should all get home as quickly as possible. Mrs. Somers will need a doctor."

"She's still unconscious." Mr. Cooper rose to his feet. "We'll have to go home by the shore and carry her. How is it to be done?"

They all looked at Trudy's rescuer, who seemed to have command of the situation.

"We'll make a stretcher." In a few moments they saw him dragging along a couple of young beech saplings stripped of their branches. Then he fetched a blanket from a recess in the cave which was slung between the beech poles. On this they placed the unconscious woman.

Meanwhile, Trudy was trying to comfort Eva.

"Cheer up, infant! We're all safe and sound, don't worry. Just think how jealous Ping will be when he hears about our adventure."

Eva consented to stem her tears.

"Yes, so he will. Mrs. Cooper saved my life, didn't she? She's very brave." Then, gazing at the burden on the stretcher. "Is my grandma dead?"

"Of course not. She'll be all right when they get her home."

Mr. Cooper and the stranger took up the stretcher between them, and Mrs. Cooper gathered Eva in her arms. "Come, darling, I'll carry you over the rocks."

Trudy was not too overcome to marvel at the mother love in her voice. The heart that had been so dead was beginning to respond again to the dictates of love.

"Trudy," said Mr. Cooper, "you will be able to get home quicker than any of us. Tell them to send for the doctor and to heat water for hot-water-bottles. Then get some dry things on."

Trudy sped away. It was a good thing to keep moving. Had she stopped to think, her nerves might have got the better of her. Soon she outstripped the others, for she had the advantage of knowing the best route to take. Obstacles were as nothing under her flying feet. Her soaked sandals rapidly dried, as did her clothes also, for the sun was warm.

The first person she caught sight of was the orra man of the farm, who was hoeing turnips in a field. She called to him to go and give the party a hand, and he left his work immediately. Miss Stewart must have seen her from the window, for she came running across the back garden, sensing that something was wrong.

Trudy gave a quick explanation:

"It was a shark . . . the boat overturned. We're all right, except for Mrs. Somers. You've to send for the doctor, and heat lots of water," she panted.

Nancy was a brick, the way she got the water ready while Miss Stewart went to the 'phone. There was a lovely big fire in the kitchen, and after she had changed, Trudy sat down beside it, comforted by the heat and the strong tea that was made for them all.

Mrs. Somers was taken up to her room and Eva was made cosy in the girls' bed with two hot-water-bottles. Mr. Cooper seemed none the worse, and his wife was a tower of strength to everyone. She seemed to think of everybody but herself.

Mr. Cooper came and stood at the fire beside Trudy, warming his hands which were blue with cold.

"Thank God we are all safe. I should never have forgiven myself if any of you had been drowned."

"But it wasn't your fault, Mr. Cooper."

"I ought to have heeded Eva's warning. What she saw must have been the fin of a shark showing above the water. There probably was a school of them. This must have been their first appearance."

"I wonder what happened to our one?"

"Probably swam off as quickly as he could, no doubt with a very bad headache."

"I didn't thank that man for saving me," Trudy remembered. "Where did he get to?"

"When the orra man came along to help us, he said he would go back and see what he could do about the boat. He seemed as if he didn't want to come near the farm."

"That's funny," remarked Trudy. "He's a pretty mysterious individual, isn't he?"

After the doctor had gone, they learned that Mrs. Somers was suffering from concussion and shock, and that she must be kept very quiet. By this time, Mr. Stewart and the orra man had gone back to Rocky Point. When they returned in the boat, which seemed little the worse, they said they had found it drawn up on the beach, but there was no sign of the red-bearded man to whom they owed so much.

There was a constant stream of people in and out of the kitchen. Olivia, who had gone for a walk after writing her letters, was much upset and alarmed when she heard what had taken place. Then David and Ping came in, eager to know all the facts. Ping was not content till every detail of the adventure had been dramatized for him. When he heard about Trudy's rescuer, his face went pink, and he stuttered excitedly:

"He's the man that lives in the c-cave, Trudy."

"That's what I suspected, but how do you know, Ping?"

"Because," he confessed, "I met him that morning I went round the shore, but he told me not to tell. It was he who gave me the compass,

Trudy. At least, he left it for me in the cave."

Trudy felt a sudden relief.

"So that's the solution. Queer goings-on, I must say. Why does he hide himself in a cave and why didn't he want to come into the house?"

The answer to these questions came to her suddenly that night after supper when she went into Mrs. Stewart's room to tell her of their adventure. As she said good-night to the invalid, she happened to glance at the picture of Donald Stewart above the organ. The face was young, and there was no beard, but there was no mistaking that pair of blue eyes, so like his mother's. At Dunglas Bay she was sure she had seen the stranger before, and she had been right. His photograph was hanging here before her.

CHAPTER XIV

The Prodigal Returns

TRUDY said nothing to anyone about her discovery. Between the excitement of the afternoon and her conjectures about Donald Stewart, she slept little that night.

It was a wonder they had escaped with their lives. She could not help dwelling on what her parents' feelings would have been if the accident had proved fatal. But God had been good to her. It was not just a blind fate that had brought Donald Stewart to the rescue in the nick of time.

What were his plans, she wondered? Did he intend to leave the island again without making himself known to his parents? That day they had met him in Dunglas Bay, he had evidently intended to board the steamer, but something had made him change his mind. It would be dreadful if he did go away without seeing his mother, who had waited all these years. It must not be allowed to happen!

She sat upright in bed. It was still early, about six o'clock in the morning; but she had made up her mind that she would go round to Rocky Point, as Ping had done, and find Donald Stewart. In any case, she would have to express her gratitude for the way he had saved her life, and if she waited till later he would probably have left the cave, perhaps for good.

Without rousing Nancy she dressed quickly and

let herself out of the house. Beyond a feeling of tiredness and lingering excitement, she was none the worse of yesterday's ordeal. How exhilarating was the air of early morning! The journey to Rocky Point, usually so laborious, presented no difficulty. Her only fear was that she would find no one at the end.

But that fear was set at rest when, rounding a bend, she saw a thin ribbon of smoke trickling upwards from the rocks. That must be his fire. He was still there!

He was placing a kettle of water on some glowing sticks, when Trudy came through the alley of rock that led to the cave.

"Good-morning!" she said brightly.

He started round, and after the first look of amazement, his white teeth flashed in a smile.

"To what do I owe the privilege of this early visit?"

"I came to say thank you," was the reply. "You saved my life, you know."

"I don't need thanks. You ought to have stayed in bed and slept off yesterday's excitement."

"I couldn't sleep. And I had to see you. You see, I know who you are."

His face became grim, and now she could see a likeness to his father.

"Who am I, then?"

"You are Donald Stewart, aren't you? There is a photograph of you in your mother's room. I recognized the likeness."

He stood very still. "You're very clever, Miss Trudy. I should be obliged if you'd keep the knowledge to yourself. I am leaving here to-day."

"No, don't go." She caught his arm, pleadingly

"If you only knew how long and how patiently your mother has waited for you to come home!"

There was a dimness in the blue eyes as he replied: "Listen, Miss Trudy, and I'll explain. As you seem to know, I ran away from home years ago, after a row with my father. I was unreasonable, I grant you, but he was more so. Lately, it came to my ears that my mother was an invalid. I came home here, thinking of nothing but seeing her again."

"And why didn't you come to see her? It would have made her so happy!"

"My nerve failed me," he replied. "I could not bear the thought of meeting my father and being ordered away again. He's a hard man, and that is the sort of thing he would do. I took shelter in this cave, where I used to play as a boy, while I made up my mind what I was going to do."

"But I don't think your father is so hard as he used to be," Trudy told him. "He gave me a rose, one day. It was the one that I passed on to you."

"I've got it yet," he said. "I knew that rose the moment I saw it on your frock. Though I meant to leave the island that day, the rose seemed to draw me back."

"I'm glad it did. I know you love your home, Mr. Donald, and I think you should take a chance and go back. Face up to your father. For your mother's sake, I'm sure he won't turn you away."

Smiling a little, he scrutinized her earnest, pleading face. "My mother has a fine champion in you, Miss Trudy. You seem to know her well."

"I do, though it's so short a time since we met. She of all people deserves happiness, and you are the one to give it to her."

Her appeal seemed to move him.

"I'd like to make her happy," he said softly. "Perhaps I shall go and see her after all."

"Oh yes, please! Do it to-day, before you change your mind. You will, won't you?"

"All right. I promise."

Trudy set off homeward, treading on air.

All forenoon, while she sat by Eva's bedside reading to her, she wondered when Donald Stewart would come to carry out his promise. When she looked into his mother's room at lunchtime, she found her kind and welcoming as before, but knew by her manner that her son had not yet appeared.

"Your eyes are very bright, to-day, my lassie. I hope yesterday's excitement wasn't too much for you?"

"Oh, no, it's not that," Trudy hastened to say.

When the others claimed her for a visit to Silver Beach, she had to consent, in case they would guess there was something in the wind. As they crossed the fields, she caught sight of Mr. Stewart mending one of the gates. He looked up and gruffed out a 'Good-afternoon.' Something about his grim face brought misgiving.

What if, after all, Donald's father ordered him off the premises? She knew so little about men and their strange, unforgiving ways.

"Go right on," she said to the others. "I want to speak to Mr. Stewart."

When she approached, he failed to look up, and Trudy lingered, her heart thumping, wondering how she was going to gain courage to speak to him. Then, with a great effort, she made herself go forward and say:

"Mr. Stewart, may I speak to you, please?"

He stopped his work, straightening his long, lean figure. "Ay, what is it?"

Not an encouraging beginning, thought Trudy. Nevertheless, she went on:

"Do you remember that rose you gave me a few days ago?"

His brow furrowed.

"It was a salmon-pink rose that had broken off its bush," she reminded him. "I took it with me to Dunglas Bay and gave it away to someone I met there."

He looked at her, puzzled. "Ay?" he said again.

"It was a man—with a red beard. He recognized the rose as coming from a bush he once knew. I saw him again yesterday, Mr. Stewart. It was he who saved my life. He's been sleeping in the cave round at Rocky Point, because—" she halted, then went on quickly—"because he's been afraid to come home."

The stern, sun-browned face flushed over a deep red.

"What's this you're telling me?" he snapped.

Trudy, trembling in her shoes, made reply:

"That man was your son, Mr. Stewart."

His face was disbelieving. "If he told you that, he was telling a lie."

"No, I'm sure he wasn't. I recognized him myself from the picture in Mrs. Stewart's room. I met him this morning and I thought it best to tell you to expect him home quite soon."

She could see his face working strangely as he pondered her words. Then:

"If it is my son Donald, he need not come back here. I told him I'd have nothing more to do with him, and I meant what I said."

So Donald had been right; his father was still unforgiving. But there was an uncertain note in his voice that held some hope, if she could only work upon it. She went up and put her hand over his hard, brown one.

"You don't really mean that, do you, Mr. Stewart? You know how happy it would make your wife if you and Donald were to be friends again."

He looked down at her young, pleading face.

"Why do you concern yourself about us, Miss Trudy? We are nothing to you."

"That's where you're wrong. I am very fond of Mrs. Stewart. No one could help admiring her for her courage and faith."

"Ay," he said tenderly, "she is a good woman. I don't know how she keeps so cheerful."

"She is helped by a strength beyond her own," Trudy told him, "and she has lived in the hope that Donald would come back. If he sees you don't want him, he will go away again, Mr. Stewart. Surely you love your wife well enough to want to make her happy?"

It took all her courage to make the appeal.

"You're a bit young to tell a man of my years what he should and should not do," he declared. "What does a girl like you know about life?"

She smiled at him.

"Not very much. But I do know that if people allow themselves to be ruled by love, they can't go very far wrong."

"You're maybe right. Ay, maybe you are right."

She was emboldened to go on. "Remember the parable of the Prodigal Son? He had treated his father badly and perhaps he didn't deserve to be welcomed home, but when his father saw him coming, he didn't take that into account; he just knew that he loved him, and he went to meet him, forgetting everything else."

"Ay, so he did. That's true, lassie." Trudy saw the old man's eyes gaze reflectively into the distance to where the green fields met the blue of the sea. She turned to follow his glance and saw a figure appear upon the horizon, a figure which moved steadily towards them, until Trudy could make out the long stride of Donald Stewart himself.

"He's coming," she said. "That's your son, isn't it, Mr. Stewart?"

He did not answer her. A change was coming over his face, softening its stern lines and suffusing it with feeling. His lips moved silently as he took a step away from her towards the approaching figure. Then he began to walk towards him, slowly at first, then breaking into a run.

When Donald saw him coming, he too hastened his steps. When they met, Trudy saw his father's arm going round his son's shoulders and remembered vividly the words of the parable:

"When he was yet a great way off, his father saw him, and had compassion, and ran, and fell on his neck and kissed him."

She turned away, tears in her eyes, and walked towards the Silver Beach. When she last saw them, Donald and his father were walking towards the house, the old man's hand still on his son's shoulder. And so another Prodigal returned and was welcomed into his father's house.

She was not privileged to see the reunion between mother and son, but what actually took place was almost exactly as she might have imagined it.

The two men went in through the back door and straight to the mother's room.

"I will go in first," the father said, "and prepare her, so that it will not be too great a shock."

He stepped softly into the room where his wife lay with her eyes closed, her Bible beside her on the pillow. She was not asleep, but meditating, as she often did, on what she had just been reading:

'Weeping may endure for a night, but joy cometh in the morning.'

She heard voices at the door, and her eyes fluttered open to see her husband standing beside her with shining eyes and a face transformed.

She raised herself on her elbow.

"I know what has happened, Andrew. Our Donald has come home at last."

He nodded. "He is here at the door. It won't be too much for you to see him, my dear?"

"It is what I have been waiting for," she replied, and at that, the big, bearded man stepped into the room and came over to the bedside. A great sob left his throat as he cast himself down on his knees beside her.

"Oh Mother, Mother!"

She put her hand on his head, as she used to do when he was small, and smoothed his hair with a gentle, loving gesture. Then her eyes met her husband's:

"We will thank God, Andrew, for what He has done for us this day."

Humbly, the old man got down on his knees, and all the hard core of him melted at last as he listened to the quavering prayer of gratitude offered up by a loving mother for the return of her son.

CHAPTER XV

Happy Hours

AFTER the memorable adventure with the
shark, the Lawsons' holiday at Ardensheel
entered a new phase. With old Mrs. Somers
upstairs in bed, where she was being tended by a
nurse from the village, and with the altered be-
haviour of Mrs. Cooper, the atmosphere of the house
was free from discord, and a spirit of cheerful
companionship existed between the guests. This
was enhanced by the presence of Donald Stewart,
whose return had been very timely, as he was able
to help with the harvest and to give his sister a hand
with the heavy work in the house. Now that father
and son were reconciled, they worked together in
complete harmony and the old man seemed much
more sociable and easier to get on with.

As for Donald, he was so happy to be home that
he went about the house singing and filling the
place with laughter. He was a boy again at heart,
a fact which Ping sincerely appreciated, as he
followed him around like a little shadow. One day
he said to him:

"I like you, Mr. Donald. I like everything about
you, except your beard."

Donald stopped chopping firewood to laugh.

"What's wrong with my beard?"

"It's frightening. It makes you look like a wild man."

"Does it, now?" He fingered his wiry chin
thoughtfully.

"That's what my sister says too. I don't believe my mother likes it either. Perhaps I'll shave it off. Let's ask your sister Trudy, shall we? She's got a lot of sense, that girl."

So Trudy was fetched, to give her opinion.

"I'm thinking of shaving off my beard, Trudy. 'To be or not to be, that is the question.' I'll abide by your decision."

Trudy regarded the bushy red growth reflectively.

"There's no doubt it's a handsome beard, Mr. Donald, but it makes you look so old! Would you mind very much if it wasn't there?"

His eyes twinkled. "Well, I might feel a bit cold, but I'd soon get used to that."

"Then you'd better shave it before the summer's over, if you're going to do it at all. I think your mother would love to see you as you used to be. If you felt it too cold, you could grow it again, couldn't you?"

Within the hour, the beard had disappeared. The change in him was wonderful. He looked almost boyish, and one could see the laughing lines of his mouth and the fine mould of his chin. Trudy was in Mrs. Stewart's room when he first appeared, and she could not help comparing him with the picture on the wall, and deciding that the years had not made much difference after all. His mother beamed on him.

"It's my own boy back again! Now you can come and kiss me properly. I never did like that jaggy old chin protector."

With a pleased laugh, he came over and gave her a bearlike hug.

"You women folk! I've given in to you about my beard, but don't think I'll be so obliging every time!"

Trudy got the impression, however, that there was nothing he would not do to make amends for his long absence. Once or twice as she passed the door, she could hear his deep voice reading aloud from his mother's Bible. These two were very close together in spirit, and it would not be long until the godly woman had guided her son into the true, worshipful way in which she herself trod. Yes, and his father as well, for although Mr. Stewart had hitherto held himself aloof from his wife's religion, his heart had been so moved on the day of his son's return that he was now willing to listen to the beautiful message of the Gospel whose inspiration had kept his wife's faith alight all those years.

This inspiration could also be detected in the attitude of Mrs. Cooper, whose calm demeanour was very different from the bitterness she had shown at the beginning. Now, as she watched them at table, Trudy could see glances of love and understanding passing between her and her husband, and often their hands would meet as if in reassurance.

It was beautiful, too, to see how the bereaved couple reacted to the lonely little Eva, whose place was now laid at their table, and whose bed was transferred to their room. They showed her all the love and sympathy that they would have given to their own child had she lived. Under their care, Eva blossomed like a flower and her gay laugh was heard echoing through the house.

Mrs. Somers' recovery from the effects of the accident was very slow and visits to her room were not encouraged by the nurse. Trudy was surprised, therefore, when one day the latter stopped her on the stair.

"Mrs. Somers has been asking for you, Miss. She would like you to go in and see her."

"But are you sure she means me?"

"Oh yes, she definitely asked for 'Trudy Lawson, the girl with the bright hair and the happy smile.'"

In spite of the description, Trudy did not hope for anything but hard words from the invalid. Knowing what her former attitude had been, she fully expected to be told off in no uncertain fashion. Probably the whole blame for the affair of the shark would be laid on her shoulders! "Well," she thought, "I might as well brace myself for it, but I do wish it was over!"

She was not prepared to see her old enemy looking so white and frail that a breath might almost blow her away. The face on the pillow was sunken and her thin hands lay lifeless on the cover, with the blue veins showing through the transparent skin. She looked like one who not so long ago had been face to face with death.

"You wanted to see me, Mrs. Somers?"

The eyes flickered open, as the reply came in a whisper:

"Is that Trudy Lawson? I have something to say to you."

Now for it, thought Trudy, but her fears had fled. This frail old woman could do her no harm. Enemy or no, Trudy felt tremendously sorry for her.

"It's about Eva. I want you to buy her a pair of sandals, like yours. And tell her . . . she can go without her socks; and it doesn't matter if she spoils her frocks . . . as long as she is happy."

The phrases came in little gasps, as if she scarcely had the strength to speak. What had caused this change in her? There was something very pathetic

about her penitent attitude. Gone was the proud,
domineering spirit against which Trudy had battled
in vain. It had been replaced by a mood of humility
and uncertainty, as if illness had disturbed all the
foundations of her being.

"I'll be very pleased to do what you wish, Mrs.
Somers. Is there anything else?"

"Yes, there is." She looked straight at Trudy
with eyes that were dim. "You are just a young
girl, Trudy, but you once said something to me
I shall never forget. When I told you that I had
never felt the need of religion, you replied that I
might come to need it yet. You were right." She
paused for breath. Her voice was so faint, Trudy
had to bend forward to catch it.

"I have been very ill, Trudy. It would have been
a terrible thing if I had died, hard and unrepentant
as I was. Lying here, with nothing to do but
think, I have come to realize that religion is the one
thing I do need. I believe I have known it all
along, but I was too proud to give in. Now I am
proud no longer. I am only too willing to listen to
anyone who can save me from—from the remorse
of conscience that haunts me day and night."

As Trudy listened to the moving confession, she
felt very young and inexperienced. Someone older
than herself was needed here. If only her mother
had been present, she would have known how best
to deal with this woman in distress.

Then, as if in answer to her wordless prayer,
she heard, through the open door, the familiar,
vibrant tones of Brian Clyde, who had just been
let into the house.

"Mrs. Somers," she said, "there is someone downstairs who can speak to you better than I can,

about the things you need. May I fetch him up to see you? His name is Brian Clyde."

The pale lips moved again.

"Perhaps he won't think it worth his while to come and see an old done woman like me."

"Yes, he will. I'm sure he will. Jesus thought everyone was worth while, and Brian is like him." She ran downstairs to the hall, where the visitor was talking to Olivia Winton.

.. "Please." Trudy caught his arm. "Will you come up and see Mrs. Somers? She is ill, and sorry, and I think you can help her."

His response was immediate. "I'll come at once. Excuse me, Olivia."

Trudy took him to the door of the room and showed him inside, leaving the two together. What transpired she could only guess at, but when later she saw Mrs. Somers, she knew by the peaceful look on her face that he had brought comfort to her repentant soul.

"It is all so simple," the sick woman whispered. "To trust in Him, to believe wholly in the words: 'I am the Way, the Truth, and the Life.' If only I had allowed myself to believe, before I became old, how much happier my life would have been!"

Trudy wondered how many more people there were like Mrs. Somers, who went on blindly, year after year, closing their ears to the voice of God and to the message of salvation, only to discover that human nature, unaided by God, must fail them in the end. Not that it was too late, even then, to call upon His goodness, but how much suffering they would have been saved had they heeded the injunction of the Scriptures: "Remember now thy Creator in the days of thy youth, while the evil days come not, nor the years draw nigh, when thou shalt say, I have no pleasure in them."

The boys lit a fire that night beside their tent and the four of them sat round it, talking in snatches as they watched the dancing flames and sniffed the gipsy perfume of the burning sticks.

Trudy told them about Mrs. Somers and her unexpected change of heart.

"Eva will be all right now. She'll have much more freedom. Her grandmother seems to understand her much better than she did. Her eyes have been opened to lots of things. It's a terrible thought, all the same, that she had to nearly die before she would relent."

"She's what you call a 'strong character'," observed David. "They can go on till doomsday without giving in. I'm surprised at her breaking down. Perhaps somebody said something to her that made her think."

"Trudy did," said Ping. "I heard her one day sticking up for the way we had been brought up to believe in Jesus."

"Bravo, Trudy. You must have managed to penetrate her iron exterior. Poor old soul, I guess it wasn't her fault she was made that way."

Here Nancy made a thoughtful observation:

"Then how is it anybody's fault when they do wrong? They can always say they were 'made that way.'"

"I dare say they can," said Trudy, "but I'm quite sure they know in their hearts that it is just an excuse. Anyhow, none of us has got any excuse, for we've been taught all our lives to distinguish right from wrong. We should be jolly thankful that we have, too."

"And we should take care not to be superior when we're dealing with less fortunate folk than ourselves," was David's reply. "I hate good people who are always looking down their noses at their 'weaker brethren.'"

"Like the publican who thanked God he was not as other men," put in Nancy. "Nasty old thing, he must have been."

As they sat in silence, David's glance went past the glowing fire to another ruby light in the west, where the sun was sinking behind the dark hills, in a glory of roseate colour.

"Look," he said, "isn't that beautiful?"

"Just like the hymn," suggested Ping. "Let's sing it now, round our camp fire."

Softly the four young voices mingled in the still evening air:

> The sun declines; o'er land and sea
> Creeps on the night;
> The twinkling stars come one by one
> To shed their light;
> With Thee there is no darkness, Lord;
> With us abide,
> And 'neath Thy wings we rest secure,
> This eventide.

CHAPTER XVI

Olivia's Wonderful Day

NOW the holiday at Ardensheel had reached the stage when the days began to fly past with breathless speed. Making the most of each precious minute, the Lawsons explored the countryside and the sea-shore, but their favourite spots were still Rocky Point and the Silver Beach.

There were frequent excursions, too, to the forenoon service at Waterside, and David often went there in the afternoons as well to paint under the guidance of Brian Clyde, and gain some priceless tuition that would help him in his future career.

Mrs. Somers was still confined to bed, but she was not lonely, for the guests took turns of sitting with her and giving her the news of the place, just as they did with Mrs. Stewart. No longer was Eva's grandmother a formidable figure, and the little girl soon lost her fear of her. Keeping her promise, Trudy journeyed into Dunglas Bay to buy a pair of sandals and a frock that would stand up to wear and tear. For Eva there ensued a time of health-giving freedom which she had never had before, and she returned with touching confidence the love which Mrs. Cooper bestowed upon her.

When the time came for the Coopers to go home, it was arranged that Eva should go with them, to stay until her grandmother was fit to look after her again. Though eager for this new experience, Eva was sorry to leave the Lawsons, especially Ping.

On the day of their departure, they all went into Dunglas Bay to see them off.   Eva sat beside Trudy in the bus.

"Perhaps my grandma will bring me back next year," said the little girl. "Will you be here, Trudy?"

"I don't know, Eva, but we'll meet again some day, I'm sure. Ping will be writing to you, won't he?"

"He said he would, but boys are awful for forgetting. Perhaps Mrs. Cooper will help me to write a letter to him. She's very good to me, and she knows about Jesus, too. If it wasn't for leaving you and Ping, I'd be so happy!"

Before boarding the steamer, the Coopers shook hands all round. Trudy had become very fond of the woman who had treated her first advances with such frigidity. Mrs. Cooper smiled warmly as she said good-bye.

"Like Eva, I am sorry to leave you all. I've been much happier here than I expected to be. Thank you for your friendship, Trudy. It has meant a lot to me."

"And to me, too," added her husband with a look of gratitude.

Ping's voice was very choky as they turned away after waving to the steamer until the tiny speck of Eva had faded into the distance.

"I'll have nobody to play with now."

"You've still got Rusty," Nancy reminded him. "And you'd rather potter around with your cave man anyway. Eva's only a little girl."

"She's quite a decent sort of girl." declared Ping; which was great praise from him.

"I suppose the Coopers will miss her a lot when

she goes back to her grandmother," remarked David.

"Yes, but they live quite near each other, so it won't be so bad," Trudy told him," and perhaps some day the Coopers might have another little girl of their own. Wouldn't it be lovely if they had?"

New guests were not expected at Ardensheel until the Lawsons had departed, so for the last day or two they and Olivia Winton were alone together.

Olivia's health had improved amazingly. She looked prettier than ever and was as full of spirits as Nancy herself. The change in her was not only in health, however. The hours she had spent pouring over Trudy's Bible and listening to the preaching of Brian Clyde were beginning to bear fruit. The tired, unhappy look in her eyes had been replaced by a sparkle which had come from increased assurance and a reborn hope.

Trudy had proof of this when she and Nancy accompanied her to Waterside on the day before their departure. They came to the place where they had to cross the now familiar stepping-stones. Olivia, without a pause, sprang lightly across, showing confidence in every step.

"There's nothing wrong with your nerves now!" laughed Trudy.

"No, I am quite cured. Brian said I would be," was tne reply.

"And to think that was less than three weeks ago!"

"Have you made any plans for when your holiday is over?" Trudy asked her.

Olivia shook her head. "Not yet. When I came here, I thought I should never have the heart to make plans again.   But now I know I shall make them, or that they will be made for me, when the time is ripe.   Isn't it strange, Trudy, that the loss of my voice doesn't worry me any more?   Somehow, I have got complete confidence in the future."

Trudy knew the reason for that.   Olivia had taken to heart the reassuring words:

'Take therefore no thought for the morrow; for the morrow shall take thought for the things of itself.   Sufficient unto the day is the evil thereof.'

There was something special in the atmosphere to-day, thought Trudy.   Whether it was the sparkle of sunshine on the silver pebbles and blue sea, or the fact that they were looking on this scene for the last time and thus were observing it more closely, she could not say.   As they approached Brian Clyde's house, the fishermen were coming out of their cottages.   Soon they were grouped together on the beach.   Trudy and her friend stood a little above the others on the grassy bank to listen to the service.

The first hymn was sung, and after Brian Clyde had put up a short prayer, he began to speak to them in the simple, heartfelt way they had grown to love.   To-day his theme was the saving power of Jesus Christ for those who were sad, despairing, and bowed down with care.   He told of the many people who, in His lifetime, were rescued from sin and hopelessness by obeying the simple command: Follow Me.   To-day, that command was still as powerful to save as when Jesus Christ was on earth, and the remedy for broken hearts and broken lives was the same now as it had been then.

Trudy noticed that Olivia was listening intently, her lustrous dark eyes on the speaker's face, her

lips slightly open in her eagerness not to miss one
word. There was such conviction in the speaker's
voice that a hush fell on the company and the
listeners were visibly moved by his pleading.
When, having concluded his talk, he asked them to
sing the well-known hymn, 'Jesus Saves,' the men's
voices rose in deep-throated fervour:

> We have heard a joyful sound—
> Jesus saves!
> Spread the gladness all around:
> Jesus saves!

Trudy became aware that Olivia had begun to
tremble, while her face was suffused with an
almost rapturous glow. Then from the open lips
from which the gift of song had been so long
absent, came a silver thread of sound, uncertain at
first, but gaining in confidence as the hymn pro-
ceeded:

> Waft it on the rolling tide:
> Jesus saves!
> **Tell** to sinners far and wide,
> Jesus saves!
> Sing, ye islands of the sea;
> Echo back ye ocean caves;
> Earth shall keep her jubilee:
> Jesus saves!

The fishermen heard it too as the beautiful voice
rose, pure and sweet, above their deeper tones.
One by one they stopped singing, to marvel and to
listen, until Olivia's voice was heard alone, filling
the summer air with the words which at last
she had come to believe, wholly and unconditionally:

> Sing above the battle's strife
> Jesus saves!
> **By** His death and endless life
> Jesus saves!—

When the service was over, Brian Clyde, his strong face working with emotion, came over to Olivia and took her by the hand. Together they walked up to his house, talking earnestly, while Trudy and Nancy waited on the beach, still full of awe for what had happened.

"She said she had lost her voice, that she would never sing again!" exclaimed Nancy.

"That was what the doctor told her. Isn't it wonderful, Nancy? A miracle, in fact."

The fishermen were talking about it too. They had never heard singing like it.

"She sang like an angel," they said. "You had to listen. It was as if it came from heaven."

They spoke the truth, thought Trudy. The renewed power to sing had come to Olivia from heaven itself.

They waited until she and Brian came from the house again after their talk. Going home, Olivia walked between them, an arm in each of theirs.

"This is the most wonderful day of my life," she told them.

"You must feel very happy to have got your voice back," said Nancy.

"Yes, I am happy about that, but not only that. It was the glorious feeling that came over me, just before I started to sing, the conviction that what Brian had said was utterly true, beyond all doubting. I want to tell the whole world, Trudy, that 'Jesus Saves.'"

Trudy pressed her arm. "I think I know how you feel. And now you won't have to worry about the future, Olivia. You'll be able to take up your career from where you left off."

But Olivia shook her head.

"No, Trudy, there's something better I can do with my voice than that. What it is I don't know yet, but I feel as if it had been given back to me for some special purpose."

They spent their last afternoon very quietly at the Silver Beach, and in the evening Trudy and Nancy went to take farewell of Mrs. Stewart, for they were leaving with the early morning bus. Olivia was there before them, sitting by the bed, and they knew she had been telling the invalid about the wonderful occurrence of the morning. Mrs. Stewart's eyes were shining.

"It is one of the things I have been praying for, that you would some day be able to sing again, but I dared not hope it would be so soon. And now, my dear Olivia, you must sing to me. Nancy will play your accompaniment on the organ."

They chose that simple and beautiful hymn of thanksgiving:

> Let us with a gladsome mind,
> Praise the Lord, for He is kind;
> For His mercies aye endure,
> Ever faithful, ever sure.

Olivia sang with a calm, shining face and a voice whose quality was both richer and sweeter than anything they had ever heard. They were so intent that they scarcely heard the door opening as Brian Clyde slipped quietly into the room to listen with the rest, his eyes intent on the singer's face.

"That was very beautiful," he murmured when the hymn was over. Then, turning to Mrs. Stewart: "The air of Ardensheel seems to be able to work some marvellous cures!"

"Aye," she replied smiling, "there's something in the air these days, right enough."

After some talk, Olivia said good-night, and Brian went out of the room with her. Nancy excused herself, saying that she had to get some recipes from Miss Stewart to take home with her, and Trudy was left alone with the old lady.

She sat down by the bed. "I'll be sorry to leave here, and to leave you, Mrs. Stewart."

"And I shall be sorry to let you go, Trudy. It has been a very happy three weeks since you came."

"Such a lot has happened in the time," was the thoughtful reply. "I'd hardly have believed it possible that people could have changed so much."

"With the Lord all things are possible," murmured the old lady.

"Even Mrs. Somers—"

"Ay. What do you think, Trudy? To-day she sent down word by the nurse that whenever she got out of bed she was coming down here to have a talk with me. I daresay a couple of old crocks like us will have plenty to say to each other!"

"Old crock, indeed," said Trudy, kissing her. "Your spirit's as young as mine is. But you will find Mrs. Somers quite human, these days. She's a much more lovable person than she was, and much happier, too."

"Everyone seems to have become happier these last few weeks. Remember the day you first came, Trudy, how gloomy this house was?"

"Yes, we all felt it, but now, as Brian said, there's 'something in the air.'"

"Ay," reflected the other, "but it didn't get there by itself. God can work marvellous changes, but He needs human instruments to work through.

During your holiday you have been an instrument of God, Trudy."

"It was you and Brian Clyde, who helped God most," whispered Trudy, as she leaned over to say good-bye. "I'm still so young, I can't do much."

"You have done more for me than I can ever say, in bringing back my son. Donald told me, you know, about how you pleaded with him to come home, and even my husband confessed that if it hadn't been for you, he might still have hardened his heart. I cannot thank you enough, my dear. May God continue to use you to bring happiness into the world," and she drew Trudy towards her, kissing her fondly with tears in her eyes.

It was with a full heart that Trudy went up to the little bedroom beneath the cam-ceiling for the last time. She smiled as she saw Nancy's dark head on the wrong pillow as usual. Nearly every night she had had to shift her to her own place at the back. To-morrow night, that would not happen, for each would have a bed of their own.

For some minutes she stood at the window watching the calm waters of the sleeping cove and the dark blue sky above. She was going to miss this scene and all these people whose lives she had shared for the last three weeks, but the memory of this holiday would be something bright to look back upon in the cold, dark days of winter.

CHAPTER XVII

Going Home

NEXT morning, Trudy opened her eyes to a sunny dawn and the chirping of birds in the trees. The fresh tang of the sea air came in at the open window, reminding her that before another day had passed, they would have travelled far from here, back to the dusty, workaday town of Drumleigh.

No girl who has a good home and loving parents to return to can wholly regret when holidays are over, and she was looking forward to the reunion and to the familiar things of home. Within a few weeks, too, she would be back at day school with her chum Esther and her old companions. Good times lay ahead and she looked forward to them with keen anticipation.

She was aware, however, of a shadow clouding the immediate future, and recollected that the time was at hand when she would have to break the news to Ping of the accident which had befallen his beloved cat, Abednego. She began to wish that she had told him the worst long ago instead of putting off the evil hour. It was going to be an unhappy journey for Ping, knowing that there would be no pet to greet him at the end of it, and she dreaded to see his eager little face clouding over when he heard the news.

Then she heard Ping himself at the door:

"Time you two lazy-bones were up!"

He popped his head into the room. "Miss Stewart says we'll have to leave the house before eight and it's nearly seven now!"

"That's all right; we're all packed," Trudy told him. "Are you glad to be going home, Ping?"

He looked doubtful. "It'll be nice to see Mum and Dad of course, but what will Rusty do without me? He'll be sure to die with loneliness. It's not so bad for me; I've got Abednego to go back to."

Poor Ping, he was going to be bereft indeed.

Trudy raised herself on her elbow to look into her little brother's face. "Keep your chin up, Ping, and get ready for a bit of bad news. Poor Abednego will not be there when you get home."

A look of pained unbelief came into his eyes. "Abednego not there? What do you mean, Trudy?"

"He was run over, Ping, just after we came here. It was nobody's fault; just one of those fast cars. You'll be brave about it, won't you?"

He gulped, and bit his lip, determined not to break down, but she could see that it cost him an effort.

"If only they had let me bring him with me, it wouldn't have happened!"

"It might, you never know."

"I'd have watched him every minute. I wouldn't have let any nasty old cars go near him. I wish I had never come here at all!"

Nancy, now awake, sat up in bed:

"Even if you'd been at home, he might still have been run over. You couldn't possible have watched him every minute. Cheer up, you'll get another cat."

Ping was indignant. "I don't want another cat! You're a heartless thing, Nancy Lawson! You've got no feelings!" So saying, he made blindly for the door, and they could hear him clattering downstairs.

Trudy got out of bed, sighing. "If only I'd told him before, he'd have got over it by now. This is going to make him unhappy all day."

When the girls came downstairs they found that Donald Stewart had collected their luggage in the hall.

"I'll get some of this stuff along to the bus while you are at breakfast." Then he saw Ping's crestfallen face. "Hello, old man, you don't seem in your usual spirits. Anything the matter?"

Trudy explained about Ping's loss.

"That's too bad." Donald laid a fatherly hand on the boy's shoulder, but even the sympathy of his hero did little to soothe his grief.

During their hurried breakfast which was shared by Olivia Winton, who was going to the bus to see them off, Ping sat in unwonted silence, eating scarcely a bite. When they had said good-bye to Miss Stewart and set off along the field path with the remainder of the luggage, Ping was the one silent member of the company.

Mr. Stewart was already at work in the field. He came forward to shake hands with the four of them, bidding them God speed. Holding Trudy's hand in his hard grip, he said:

"Come back again, lass. We owe you a lot. You've been a real ray of sunshine in this place!"

Promising to do her best to return, Trudy walked on with Olivia. Her friend was looking radiant this morning.

"Before we say good-bye, Trudy, I've got something to tell you. Brian and I are going to be married!"

The news took Trudy's breath away, though it was true that she and Nancy had once or twice discussed the growing friendship between these two, hoping it might lead to this happy conclusion.

"Oh, Olivia, how lovely! You must be very, very happy."

Nancy had overheard, and added her congratulations. "It just gives a lovely finishing touch to the holidays, doesn't it?"

"It does for me, I know," laughed Olivia.

"And yet, it seems a pity too, after you getting your voice back."

"Oh, my voice won't be wasted. Brian and I had a long talk about that last night. I think you know, Trudy, that Brian has plans to start a winter mission, moving about from town to town, wherever he feels he is needed. He is sure he can do a lot of good that way, and I am going with him. He thinks my singing will have an effect on people. that it will help to bring God into their lives."

Trudy felt that Brian was right. "It's a wonderful idea. I'd love to be there some time, Olivia, to hear him speak and you sing. Do you think you might visit Drumleigh?"

"It's more than likely. I'll let you know, Trudy. I've got your address and shall certainly write."

Her words took the sting out of the coming parting, for now that there was a chance of seeing Olivia again, Trudy could leave her with a good heart. Their scheme sounded an ideal one, full of possibilities for good. That two gifted people like Brian and Olivia should sacrifice all worldly aims to devote their lives to this cause, was a splendid and ennobling gesture which would be sure to appeal to their audiences as much as it did to Trudy herself.

David heard the news with mixed feelings. Though he held the same views as Trudy that the mission would be a fine undertaking, he saw Brian Clyde as an artist rather than a preacher.

"He won't give up his painting, will he?"

"No," said Olivia, "he can't do that. Where would our bread and butter come from? In the summer we shall come back to Waterside, and he will be able to paint there."

When they came near the bus stop, they found Donald Stewart waiting for them. A series of sharp barks told them that Rusty was with him. He did not come to meet them, because Donald held him on a lead.

"Hello, Rusty." Ping's voice sounded very flat. "I wondered where you had got to." As Rusty jumped up to lick his hands, he fondled the dog's head sadly. "Why did you bring him, Mr. Donald? I'd rather have gone away without seeing him. Good-byes are such sad things!"

He was very near to tears. Trudy's heart was sore for him. But Donald put a comforting hand on his shoulder.

"You don't need to say good-bye, Ping! You can take Rusty with you. That's why I brought him. He wants to come, I can see that!"

"You mean for keeps?"

"Certainly; with Trudy's permission. Will it be all right, Trudy?"

She nodded, overcome. How thoughtful of Donald to realize that this present was the one way of making Ping forget his loss!

"Thank you millions," gasped Ping, hugging the puppy to him in an ecstasy of joy.

"He always wanted a dog of his own, even

before he got Abednego," explained Trudy. "We can never thank you enough."

"The debt is still on our side," said Donald gravely.

They could hear the bus approaching from the village and were preparing to say farewell, when a shout reached them, and there was Brian Clyde running towards them across the fields.

"Glad I'm not too late to see you off!" he said as he came up. "You people who go away at the crack of dawn make things very difficult for sleepy-heads like me!"

But he looked anything but a sleepy-head as he shook hands with the four Lawsons. He had a special word for David as the bus came in.

"If you ever want to consult me about anything, write to me at Waterside and the letters will be forwarded. Olivia and I will have no abiding city for most of the year, isn't that so, Olivia?" He looked down at his sweetheart fondly.

"In a way, yes," Olivia replied. Trudy guessed she meant that her 'abiding city' was by his side, wherever they might be.

Helped by the three grown-ups they got aboard, Ping's attention wholly taken up with Rusty who was not too sure about the bus as a place for dogs.

Trudy's last glimpse as the vehicle rattled off, was of Brian and Olivia standing arm-in-arm waving vigorously, and Donald Stewart beside them looking rather wistful as he gave his parting salute.

In what seemed a very short time, they arrived at Dunglas Bay, where they boarded the morning steamer. The day was fine and warm and they were able to sit up on deck watching the shore line of their beloved island getting more remote as they sailed away.

"Well, that's the end of our holiday," declared David, looking glum.

"I don't think it is," said Trudy. "Nothing is ended that you can still remember."

Nothing is ended, she might have said, that helps to develop and enrich one's personality. Though not able to express it in that way, each of them felt that something good had been added to their lives.

For Ping, there was the memory of his cave-man, the friendship of Eva, and his new pet, Rusty, who lay curled up beside him on the seat, adoring puppy eyes following his every movement. Nancy would take with her into her future life the mellow sound of Mrs. Stewart's old organ, and the new domestic skill which had come to her from Miss Stewart's practical tuition, while David would never forget the thrill of being at home in Brian Clyde's studio; and his career would be not a little affected by the things he had learned from him.

Trudy had much to remember, too, perhaps more than any of them, because she had the gift of penetrating into the deeper meaning of things. At Ardensheel they had found a group of unhappy people whose lives were bringing nothing but discord to themselves and to others. All these people had had problems of totally different kinds, but—and this was the wonderful thing—they had all been solved, and their lives had been healed by the same unfailing remedy—the love of God and the saving power of His Son, Jesus Christ.

Though she had still a lot to learn, Trudy knew enough about the world to realize that every corner of it was ridden by the same evils as the house at Ardensheel—pride, selfishness, lost hopes, determined blindness to everything outside the material world. Would the same remedy that had worked so miraculously at Ardensheel work all over the world, if people could only be brought to believe in it? Yes, she was sure it would. And just as she had been instrumental in bringing harmony at Ardensheel, so she could go on working for Christ, quietly and persistently, wherever she might find herself in the years to come.

The puppy licked her hand, and she patted his smooth, brown head:

"We'll soon be home now, Rusty!"

Ping's blue eyes lit up at the prospect and David and Nancy smiled happily, for however much young folk enjoy a holiday, the thought of home is a powerful magnet to draw them back again.